"It's him," Lily said. "He sent me another text. It's from a different account but it's our guy."

"What does it say?"

She looked down at her phone and then back up and then back down again. "Next time I won't miss." She handed the phone to him so he could read it for himself.

Rex nodded. "Just as I suspected. His fixation is growing stronger and stronger with each passing day that he hasn't accomplished his ultimate goal."

"We have to make sure that he never reaches that goal. And we also need to try to stop him before he goes on killing other women on his list."

"Agreed, but you know that's much easier said than done."

The phone chirped again. "Oh no," she said. "What is it now?"

Since he still had her phone in his hand, he opened the second message. Well, that was strange. He hadn't expected this twist.

"It's a picture of you."

Rachel Dylan writes inspirational romantic suspense. Although a Georgia girl at heart, she traded in the sunny South for the snowy Midwest. She lives in Michigan with her husband and five furkids—two dogs and three cats. She's an animal lover and enjoys adding furry friends to her stories. You can find Rachel at racheldylan.com.

Books by Rachel Dylan

Love Inspired Suspense

Out of Hiding
Expert Witness
Picture Perfect Murder

PICTURE PERFECT MURDER

RACHEL DYLAN

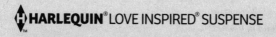

HARLEQUIN® LOVE INSPIRED® SUSPENSE

 LOVE INSPIRED BOOKS

ISBN-13: 978-0-373-44739-8

Picture Perfect Murder

Copyright © 2016 by Rachel Dylan

Printed in U.S.A.

For we walk by faith, not by sight.
−2 Corinthians 5:7

For Susan—through all the years, the ups and downs, the joy and pain, you've been there through it all.

ONE

The loud barking didn't rouse Lily Parker from a deep sleep. No, she was still wide-awake even though her head had hit the pillow an hour ago. Sleep didn't come easily, because of the recurring nightmares involving her last mission with the CIA. The mission that had changed her entire life.

Her bedroom was dark, and she glanced over at the bright red numbers on her alarm clock. She'd been working late in her darkroom developing her latest photographs, so seeing that it was three in the morning wasn't much of a surprise.

"Grace," she yelled out to her yellow Labrador. But Grace kept barking loudly downstairs. She'd rescued Grace from an animal shelter in a rough part of Atlanta six months ago. Clearly her dog hadn't gotten the memo that it wasn't acceptable to bark in the middle of the night.

"Okay, I'm coming." Reluctantly, Lily threw back the down comforter, leaving the warmth of her bed, and stood up. She grabbed her fuzzy robe from the navy chaise in the corner and walked out of her bedroom. Grace's barking only grew more persistent.

When Lily was almost at the bottom of the stairs, she thought she heard something that couldn't have come from Grace. She paused for a moment, debating whether she should run back up the steps to grab her Glock from the nightstand.

However, as a former CIA agent, she wasn't easily rattled. Knowing Grace, she'd probably become fixated on a tree branch, a possum or even something as silly as a bag blowing in the wind. She proceeded down the rest of the stairs and flipped the switch for the hallway light. But no light came on. She stepped into the pitch-black living room and suddenly felt she wasn't alone. Was someone in her house?

Grace ran into the room, almost knocking her over. "Easy, girl." She reached down and gave Grace a quick pat on the head, trying to reassure her. Taking a deep breath, she started walking toward the kitchen. At least there she could grab a knife to protect herself. She was fairly certain that she'd set the alarm before she went to bed, but now she started second-guessing herself. She'd been so engrossed in her work she couldn't remember.

Another loud bark from Grace had Lily moving quickly through the kitchen. Even though it was dark, there was still a thread of moonlight coming in through the kitchen windows. Enough light for her to locate her butcher block and grab the biggest knife she had.

Lily knew she wasn't like most women. She'd spent

five years in the CIA on highly dangerous operations overseas. But she'd never confronted danger in her own home. Although she wasn't afraid, she was angry at the possibility that someone had dared to invade her privacy. She clenched the knife in her right hand, ready to fight off any attacker.

Then she reached into the kitchen drawer, grabbed a flashlight with her left hand and scanned the bright light over the living room. Nothing.

Was it possible that there was just a power outage in the area? Possible, yes, but that wouldn't explain Grace's incessant barking. Grace stood beside her, now on high alert. The young Labrador was loyal and courageous, even if she still needed a bit of training.

Lily had had enough. She wanted to end this. "I'm calling the cops right now," she said loudly. "So you better get out of my house or show yourself, you coward."

She didn't have a landline, and her cell phone was in her bedroom. But the intruder didn't know that. Assuming there was an intruder. For a moment, she strained to listen but couldn't hear any noise now. She took a few steps back into the kitchen.

The lights flickered on and her microwave beeped, signaling the return of power to her house. Quickly, she ran up the steps to grab her gun from the nightstand, just to be on the safe side. Then she intended to clear the house room by room, as she had done many times before on missions.

But first she grabbed her cell and dialed 911, reporting to the operator that there was an intruder and she needed help right away. While she felt she could hold her own, she wasn't an idiot and would welcome some backup right now. Then her lights turned off again. Something was definitely wrong.

She quickly gave her address to the operator. She heard a sound behind her one second too late. Strong arms grabbed on to her, ripping her phone out of her hand. She didn't hesitate to act. Using years of self-defense and martial arts training, she was able to break his initial hold. Her response seemed to catch him off guard. He must've assumed that she would be a pliant victim. This man had no idea what she was capable of. He'd picked the wrong house to break into tonight.

It was dark in her bedroom, but she could see the outline of her assailant. She mentally cataloged what she could discern of his physical appearance. Male, approximately six feet tall and wearing a dark ski mask. She couldn't even get a good look at his eyes because she was too busy fighting him off.

She landed a hard right kick into his side, and he grunted loudly in pain. Not waiting for him to recover, she steadied herself into position and got in one more strong kick that made him stagger backward a few steps.

"The cops will be here any minute," she told him. Backup was on the way. But instead of what she was used to, other CIA agents backing her up—or stabbing her in the back—this would be the police.

She reached for the Glock from inside the bedside table drawer as her attacker took a few more steps back and then turned to run. He must have realized that the police had to be close to her house by now.

With the gun in her hands, she ran out of her room after him. He deserved to be arrested and face justice for what he'd done. Because if he'd done this to her, chances were he was a repeat offender.

But as she started down the stairs, she twisted her ankle and hit the ground hard. She groaned loudly. The attacker was going to get away. And there was nothing she could do about it.

FBI special agent Rex Sullivan looked over at Atlanta Police Department officer Sean Bishop, who had offered to give him a ride home. The FBI had been called in last week because the APD felt they had sufficient evidence to indicate that a potential serial killer was on the loose. Rex had been picked up earlier at the FBI field office and taken to the latest crime scene.

The woman's body had been discovered that afternoon, but she definitely hadn't been killed today. Due to the advanced state of decomposition, the coroner was placing the time of death at about two weeks ago. The victim had lived alone in a rental condo. Sadly, no one had reported the young woman missing, and it took her rent not being paid before the landlord entered the condo to find her lifeless body.

Another innocent victim of a totally heinous crime. Profiling and catching these twisted criminals was Rex's specialty. The perpetrators were most often male. And they typically possessed a lethal combination of the ability to blend in with society and the skills to be a cold-blooded killer.

The young officer with him was trying to hold it together after visiting the grisly murder scene that the FBI and APD were working together. But with the images fresh in his mind, Rex had to admit that he didn't look forward to going to bed, either. So when an emergency call had come across the radio a few minutes ago, Rex was actually relieved that they were close to the location where it came from.

"Thanks for understanding," Sean said.

"Totally understand. And I won't do anything to interfere. This is your jurisdiction." Rex was just happy to have the diversion.

"We don't even know the full details yet. Just that there was a distress call from a female citing a possible intruder and then the 911 operator lost contact. We'll be there soon, but back to today's crime scene for a minute, this makes murder number three in two months all with a similar MO," Sean said. "This guy doesn't show any sign of stopping. I'm guessing that after tonight, the FBI will officially label this guy a serial killer, right?"

Rex rubbed his chin. "I'm leaning toward that assessment, yes. We have three victims so far. All the women in their mid to late twenties, all living alone. All three of the victims had long, dark hair and light-colored eyes. But beyond that, my team is going to be working on finding other connections between the victims. It will be important to determine if there are ties between them or if he's just targeting randomly based upon looks."

Sean pulled the police car to a stop in front of the designated address. A two-story house with a big front porch. "This is it. Let's go check it out."

Rex didn't normally work active scenes. He was usually called in after the fact, once a murder had been committed. But he had finished at the top of his class at Quantico and had seen some heavy field action in his first couple of years. So he felt more than prepared to go in, and there was no way he was sending Sean into this house without backup.

They ran up the porch steps and entered the front door, which had been left unlocked. That first tidbit of information already had Rex uneasy.

"Atlanta Police. Anyone here?" Sean yelled.

Rex was met with a barking yellow Lab running full steam ahead, fur flying. The dog jumped up and put its paws on him. It seemed friendly but agitated. Probably from whatever had happened at the house. "It's okay," he told the Lab. "We're here to help."

"I'm up here," a female voice yelled loudly.

Rex followed the voice to the top of the stairs. And that was when he saw her. A beautiful woman with long, wavy, dark hair and bright blue eyes. A chill shot down his arm when he realized that she looked astonishingly like his other three murder victims.

"I'm Special Agent Rex Sullivan with the FBI, and this is Officer Sean Bishop with the Atlanta Police Department."

Sean crouched down beside her on the stairs. "The ambulance is on its way, ma'am. What happened?"

"I was attacked," she said. "The man got away."

"What's your name?" Rex asked.

"Lily Parker."

Just then, Rex's good buddy, Atlanta police detective Derrick McKinley, walked up the steps. "I heard the call for backup and I came over."

"What hurts?" Rex asked.

"My ankle," she responded. "I twisted it when I was trying to go after the guy."

"Wait. You were going after him?" Rex asked. This woman had guts.

"Yes. My Glock is right there."3 She nodded down to the step just below her. "It's mine. He knew that I'd made the 911 call. Once he couldn't easily subdue me, he probably decided to cut his losses and get out of here."

The EMT walked up the steps and went to work on Lily.

"We'll let you get medical attention," Rex said. "But then we'll need your detailed statement."

She nodded. "Absolutely. Whatever you need."

"My recommendation would be to transport her to the hospital. The doctors will need to take X-rays to determine if her ankle is broken," the paramedic said.

"I think it's just a mild sprain, if that," she said.

"Still, you need to get it looked at," he responded.

She gave a reluctant nod. "All right."

The Labrador walked up a few steps and barked, getting Rex's attention. It looked up at Rex with big chocolate-brown eyes. "What's your name, buddy?" He leaned down and took a close look at the collar with a bone-shaped nameplate hanging off it. The green collar didn't give away the gender. But the name did, along with a closer inspection of the pup.

"That's Grace," Lily said loudly from a few steps up. "She will be fine here while I'm at the hospital. I'm sure I won't be gone too long," Lily said.

Rex nodded. His mind went into overdrive analyzing the situation. It was entirely possible that this beautiful, mysterious Glock-carrying woman had just escaped being the fourth victim of a serial killer.

Lily awoke feeling completely disoriented but was quickly able to determine by the antiseptic smell that she was in a hospital. She recalled having been given a pain pill in the early-morning hours, even though she'd insisted that she didn't really need it. But the doctor wanted to get the swelling down and had said it would make her more comfortable.

Looking around the space, her heart immediately warmed. Sitting in the hospital room were two of her friends from childhood. She'd become close with them again since she'd returned to Atlanta.

"Lily, you're awake!" Alison Cruz said. Her petite, brunette friend squeezed her hand tightly and had tears in her eyes.

"How long have I been out?"

"Not that long. It's just about eleven in the morning," Jackson Bray said. She'd known Jackson since sixth grade. His dark brown eyes were filled with concern. "Guy wanted to be here, but he couldn't get anyone to cover his shift at work. We are so glad to see you awake."

"What actually happened to you? How did you hurt your ankle?" Alison asked. "We couldn't get any specific information from the police officers or the hospital. We only found out you were here because we got concerned when you wouldn't answer any of our calls or texts. So we went by your house and a police officer filled us in."

Before Lily could respond, the man she recognized as FBI special agent Rex Sullivan entered the room. Standing at least six foot two, he was dressed in a dark suit with a navy tie. His brown hair was cut short.

"Ms. Parker, how are you feeling today?" Rex asked.

"A little groggy from the pain meds, but my ankle isn't hurting as badly this morning."

"I'm glad to hear that. I'd appreciate it if I could have some time alone with you to get a full statement."

"Anything you need to say can be said in front of my friends."

He nodded. "I understand your feelings, but it's protocol."

Relenting, she looked over at Alison and Jackson. "I'm sorry, you two. Could you give us a few minutes?"

"Of course," Jackson said. He gently touched her shoulder. "We'll go grab some coffee and come back in a bit." Her friends walked out of the hospital room, leaving her alone with Rex.

He took a seat and pulled out a notepad. "I just wanted to hear your full account of what happened last night. I'm working your case in conjunction with the Atlanta Police Department."

She wondered why he'd be involved at all in a breaking and entering with an assault, but figured she would just go ahead and get this over with. "My dog Grace started barking around 3:00 a.m. I went downstairs to check things out. The power kept cutting off and on multiple times before you got there. I didn't see anyone in the house, but I felt as if someone could've been there."

"What else can you tell me?"

"I ran upstairs to get my cell to dial 911. I started making the call, and a man grabbed me before I could get to my Glock."

"Yes, we took the Glock into evidence." He paused. "What happened after he grabbed you? Did you see him?"

"It was dark in my bedroom. I estimate that he was about six feet tall, two hundred pounds, give or take. But he was dressed all in black and wore a ski mask. I couldn't even see his eyes. However, I was able to fight him off."

He nodded. "Are you trained in self-defense techniques?"

"Yes, I am. If you want my honest assessment, I think he was actually surprised I fought back. He seemed thrown off by it. And when I reminded him that the cops were coming, he started to retreat. I got my Glock and was going to go after him, but that's when I twisted my ankle and fell on the stairs."

He kept jotting down notes. "What do you do for a living, Ms. Parker?"

Here came the tricky part. Would he believe that she was a photographer? The problem was that he'd seen the Glock at the scene, so there was no escaping that. "I'm a photographer."

"That's your only job?"

"Yes. It keeps me fully occupied." Which was the truth. It was her only current job. She'd left the CIA life behind.

"Do you know anyone that would want to hurt you?"

She kept a straight face. "Not that I know of." There was no way she was divulging her CIA backstory to a man she'd just met, even if he was working her case.

He took a breath and stopped writing. "I don't want to frighten you by telling you this, but I feel I have to."

Her heartbeat sped up. "Tell me what?"

"I'm working in conjunction with the Atlanta Police Department, and we are investigating a string of murders that have occurred in the city."

"String of murders? Are you talking about a serial killer? I was wondering why the FBI was responding to a police call."

"I was working a crime scene not far away from your home when the 911 call came in last night."

"Okay, but how do I fit into all of this?"

"Once again, there's no cause for alarm at the moment. You're safe."

She nodded. "I understand. But please tell me what it is you're trying to say."

"Ms. Parker, here's the situation. You look strikingly similar to the other three victims from the case. I'm assuming you're in your twenties?"

"Yes, I'm twenty-seven."

"You live alone?"

"Yes, just with Grace."

"All of the victims have been attractive women in their twenties, living alone, with long dark hair and light-colored eyes."

She felt her eyes widen. "Seriously?"

"Unfortunately, yes."

"Are you trying to say that the attacker was in my house trying to make me his next victim? That the man I came into contact with actually may be the serial killer that you're trying to apprehend?"

"I can't say with certainty that your attacker is the same man I'm trying to hunt down, but I don't really believe in this many coincidences. The last victim was murdered approximately two weeks ago. You may have very well been his next target."

"Wow." She thought she'd left her life of danger behind when she quit the Agency.

She blew out a breath. "By any chance, did you find my cell at the house? The man who attacked me grabbed it away from me last night in the struggle."

"We didn't. Did you have any sensitive information on there like financial records—anything like that?"

"No." Her time at the CIA had taught her to be wary of storing any intel on electronic devices. "But it did have a lot of my photos on it. Things I needed for work."

"I'm sorry about your phone. We will attempt to track it, but I'm assuming that search will come up empty. I also suggest you get your locks changed."

"Thanks. That's a good idea." She looked up and saw another man walk into her hospital room. She recognized him as one of the officers at the scene last night. He screamed law enforcement, with his dark, conservative suit. He was tall with thick, blond hair.

Rex looked at her. "Ms. Parker, I don't think you officially met Derrick last night. This is Detective Derrick McKinley from the Atlanta Police Department. He's also working your case."

Derrick walked over and smiled. There was a kindness in his blue eyes. "How are you doing, Ms. Parker?"

"I'm ready to get out of here."

"I can only imagine how you must be feeling. I just wanted to stop by and check on you. And to pick up this guy." He nodded toward Rex. "The doctor said she was about to come in. Have you given Rex your statement?"

"Yes." She looked over at Rex. "Did you have more questions?"

"Not at the moment, but I'm going to need to talk with you again to determine if there is any connection between you and the previous victims. Also, we've got an APD officer here at the hospital who will escort you home."

The implication was clear. Rex thought that she may still be in danger, and she couldn't object because she needed to seem like a photographer. Not a CIA agent fully capable of defending herself. She already knew that Rex was a bit suspicious of her having a Glock. And chasing after the guy. But she felt it was better to be straightforward in her statement to him. She knew all too well about how lies could start to spiral out of control.

Lily thanked both men again, and they walked out of the room as the doctor came in. She wore wire-frame glasses and her blond hair was pulled back in a bun. "Ms. Parker, I'm Dr. Grady. How are you feeling today?"

"Ready to get out of here."

"Good news about your ankle. Not even a sprain. Just might be a little sore but shouldn't slow you down too much. I also conducted a thorough physical exam and was unable to detect any trauma. But how are you feeling emotionally? If you need to talk to anyone, we have a full staff of psychologists."

No way was she doing that. "I'm fine, Doctor. Just anxious to be home."

She smiled. "I understand that." She paused. "Ms. Parker, one other thing. An envelope was delivered for you." The doctor pulled the small envelope out of her jacket. "It might be best if you involve the police, given the circumstances. But I thought I'd talk to you about it first in case you were expecting something."

She wasn't. But she didn't want to discuss this with the doctor. "Oh, yes, it's probably from my friend who couldn't get off work this morning."

"Okay, then. It will just take the nurse a few minutes to process your discharge paperwork."

"Thank you."

Once the doctor left the room, she quickly opened the envelope. The words typed on the small card stared back at her.

```
Next time you'll be mine.
```

Her heart dropped. Was the FBI agent right? Could she have been the serial killer's latest target?

TWO

Lily settled down on her couch, snuggling up with Grace to watch the local evening news. It had been two days since the incident, and she was still on high alert after receiving that note. But she was skeptical about bringing in the police or FBI at this juncture. She didn't want anyone snooping into her life, because that would inevitably lead to questions about her past. Questions she really didn't want to answer.

How could she explain to law enforcement, those who lived and worked in between the lines, that her previous career had forced her to work outside them?

Yesterday she had gotten her locks changed and bought a new Glock—two, in fact. Along with a new phone, since the police presumably hadn't been able to locate hers. If this guy was coming after her again, she'd be ready this time. She'd been doing a lot of thinking about the past few weeks. There had been a couple of times when she was out shooting photos that she'd felt she was being watched. But she'd chalked that up to her CIA paranoia. She'd left the Agency and the life that went along with it, but she couldn't leave behind the training.

If she were being truthful with herself, she'd admit that she had enjoyed the challenge of being a CIA agent. But it was too painful to go there right now. She'd only been out for nine months.

She turned up the volume on the TV so that she could hear it over Grace's snoring. The blonde TV anchor didn't smile tonight as she looked into the camera with serious hazel eyes. "Good evening, everyone. Breaking news tonight. The FBI has officially declared that there is a serial killer roaming the streets of Atlanta. Four young women, all in their twenties, have been murdered over the past two months. The latest victim was found just last night by local police, and officials are estimating that she was killed yesterday. The FBI has gone on record to say that they, too, are on the hunt to bring justice to those who have been slain."

A shiver coursed through her body. Then the TV shot cut to a face she was familiar with—Special Agent Rex Sullivan. "We're asking everyone in the area to be vigilant. All four murders took place inside the city, but there's nothing saying that the killer will stick to his pattern. I would especially urge young women to remember that a serial killer may not look dangerous. He may come up to you in the grocery store parking lot and try to help you load bags into your car. He may approach you on a college campus. There are many different ways that a contact could occur, and I am advising everyone in the community to be on alert. If you see anything suspicious, please report it to the local police or the FBI field office in Atlanta immediately."

As the news anchor picked up the reporting, Lily's thoughts shifted to her situation. This man they were talking about might have been in her home with the intent to make her his next victim. And then it dawned on her that after he had failed with her, he'd gone out and found another innocent woman. The thought made her sick.

Her eyes went back to the screen, and she felt her mouth drop open. She reached for the remote and quickly pushed the volume up even louder. Blinking a few times, she stared at the TV.

"And tonight we have a WNB Atlanta exclusive. The photograph you are seeing was left at the latest murder scene, a fact that has been confirmed to us by the FBI. If anyone watching has information with regard to this photograph please contact the number on the bottom of your screen for the FBI field office in Atlanta immediately."

She jumped up from the couch and walked into the kitchen, trying to remember where she had put Rex's business card.

After locating it in one of the drawers, she grabbed her cell from the counter and dialed the number printed there.

After two rings, he answered. "Agent Sullivan."

"Hi. This is Lily Parker."

"Hey, Lily. How are you doing?"

"Not too good."

"I'm sorry about that. It's not uncommon to have difficulty after dealing with an attack in your own home. The Bureau has a lot of resources if you would like a referral to someone you can talk to about what happened to you."

She could hear papers shuffling around in the background. "No, please listen to me. You need to come over to my house right now. I have to talk to you."

"Are you okay?"

"Your serial killer case. I need to talk to you about that now."

"Okay. Did you think of something else that happened the night you were attacked? I can be on my way to your place in just a few minutes, but what is this about?"

"That photograph that was just televised on the local news. Is the reporting on the photo legitimate?"

"Unfortunately, yes. That photograph was found at the scene of the latest murder. The killer struck again yesterday. We found the body last night and the photo along with it."

She took a deep breath. "Agent Sullivan, I shot that photograph."

Rex sped all the way from his office, where he'd planned on working a late night, to Lily's house. A million thoughts raced through his mind, including why the killer would use one of Lily's photographs.

He also couldn't get a good read on Lily. He'd run some background checks on her and found some holes that he couldn't fill. Plus, it concerned him that she had gone after the killer when he'd attacked her. That wasn't something most people would've done under the circumstances. But even given all the question marks about Lily, she wasn't the problem. She was a potential target. The killer had zoned in on her and used her photograph to send some type of message.

Lord, more innocent women are going to be killed if I can't figure this out. Please guide me and give me strength. Rex couldn't imagine going through life without God. Especially in his line of work, where he dealt with some of the most evil people out there.

After fighting through Atlanta traffic on the interstate, he pulled into Lily's driveway. He rang the doorbell and heard Grace's loud bark. He couldn't help but smile. He really liked that dog. If he didn't work such crazy hours, he'd have one, too, but it just didn't seem fair given his lifestyle right now.

The front door opened and Lily stood on the other side. Her coloring was back to normal now, and her bright blue eyes didn't break contact with his. "Come on in."

He walked through the front door and was greeted by a very excited Grace. He knelt down for a moment to say hello.

"She really likes you," Lily said.

"I love dogs." He gave Grace another pat before he stood up.

"They're great. I'm so glad I have her here with me. Come on into the living room, and I'll try to explain everything."

The yellow Lab followed him closely as he walked into the living room and sat down in a big beige chair. Lily took a seat on the navy couch across from him, and Grace jumped onto it to join her.

"Why don't we just get right to it and you tell me about the photo," Rex said.

"All right. When I saw the news tonight, I instantly recognized the picture that they put up. I'd taken it at Westlake Park only a couple of weeks ago. I remember thinking the scene was pretty amazing. That photo was black-and-white, but I have a digital color version, too."

He leaned forward. "So first things first. You're certain that's your photo?"

"Absolutely. There's no doubt in my mind."

"And how did you take the photo?"

"With actual film. I do a combination of traditional and digital photography. But for the specific photo they showed on TV, I used film. I have a darkroom here on the first floor down the hall. I had been developing those photos the night I was attacked."

Rex frowned as he tried to process this information.

"What's wrong?" she asked.

"Just trying to put together a plausible scenario for what happened here at your house. The killer cuts your lights, breaks in and attacks you. You fight him off and he retreats, taking your phone and the photo from the darkroom."

She nodded. "Instead of being able to make me his next victim, I messed up his plan."

"When he failed to kill you, he found another innocent victim. But he still had your photo. And he decided to use it at the scene of his fourth murder. Have you looked to see if any other photos are missing?"

"Not yet. I haven't even gotten that far in my thought process." She took in a deep breath. "But I had photos on my phone, too. They weren't high quality, just images of places I wanted to go back to with my camera."

"That's good to know. I'd like to look in your darkroom and get the team out here to do additional evidence collection."

"Sure. There's another thing that I need to tell you about."

A knot formed at the pit of his stomach. "What?"

"You're not going to be happy about this, but a note was delivered to me at the hospital."

"What? What did the note say?"

"It said, 'Next time you'll be mine.'"

"Why in the world didn't you tell us about this immediately?" he asked in a raised voice.

"I didn't realize how this was all going to unfold. I'm sorry."

"Do you still have the note? We need to run prints on it and do an analysis."

"Yes, I've got it. It's in the kitchen."

"You should've told the police about this. From here on out, you have to be straight with me, Lily. Lives are literally on the line and we're up against the clock to find the killer before he strikes a fifth time."

"I understand. It won't happen again. I realize this

is a serious situation. The last thing I want is to hamper your investigation. I don't want another woman killed by this guy."

Now he had to lay something else on her, but he thought she could handle it. He was getting the very distinct impression that it would take a lot to rattle Lily Parker. "I'm not trying to alarm you, but when I examine all the facts, I think that you could still be in danger."

"Why is that?"

"You were on the killer's list of victims, but you managed to stop him. I can imagine a scenario in which he becomes obsessed with finishing the job because—let's face it—you're the one that got away. He took your photograph and placed it at the next murder scene. He also communicated with you directly via that note. I suspect he'll come after you again."

"Your theory makes sense."

He wanted to know more from her, but he needed to be careful. If he pushed too much, she might clam up. He needed as much information from her as she was willing to share. But he'd been an FBI agent long enough to know that this woman was hiding something. How many free-spirited photographers carried Glocks and seemed more annoyed than terrified at a home invasion?

"Let me show you the darkroom," she said.

He followed her down the hallway. Once they entered the room, he surveyed the area, but nothing seemed out of place. There was a big table with large plastic containers on top of it. A sink, surrounded by shelves housing numerous bottles of liquids, sat in a corner. Then there were clips and other supplies scattered throughout. "And what about your digital photography?"

"I do that in my office across the hall. That's where my computer and printer are."

"I'll need you to go through the darkroom and your computer and see if it looks as if anything else has been tampered with."

"I understand. I'll definitely do that."

"And I'm going to call the crime lab and have them do another sweep for prints just in case they missed anything, as well as run a forensic analysis on your computer. They can also collect the note for examination. Excuse me for a second." He pulled out his phone and made a quick call to his team. "They'll be here within the hour. How many pictures do you estimate were on your phone?"

She blew out a breath. "Maybe a hundred, two hundred. But like I said, they aren't top quality like the ones on my computer and in the darkroom."

He didn't like this at all. The serial killer had access to more of Lily's photographs. And if he was going to start using photos as part of his deadly game, then the implications were staggering. Rex didn't even want one more death on his watch, but the killer obviously had other, bigger plans.

"Agent Sullivan, you're off in another world, aren't you?"

"Please, call me Rex. And I'm sorry. When I get

into a case, my mind goes into overdrive trying to connect the dots."

She looked down and back up at him, her blue eyes sparkling. "Why would this guy focus on me of all people?"

"Because he has a distinct type. You meet all of his preselected physical requirements. We can't know at this point why he chose to go after women who look like you. I'm going to coordinate with APD so we can figure out what makes sense for some sort of protective detail. Meanwhile, I'll stay with you until the FBI team arrives. Then I'll come back tonight."

Frowning, she walked out of the darkroom, and he followed her back to living area. "That's not necessary. My friends you met at the hospital are coming over soon. I won't be alone."

"Okay, but if that changes let me know. I'm also going to put FBI electronic surveillance in place. That should be set up by tomorrow."

She winced as she took a seat on the sofa. "Is that really necessary at this point? That's a pretty aggressive approach."

"It is, but I think it's needed. We have no idea how far this guy is going to take it with you. I find it deeply disturbing that he's come after you once and has used your photo at a murder scene. I don't take this threat lightly."

"I have one request for you."

"Sure. What do you need?"

"I don't want my name to be associated with this photo in the news."

"I understand. It's not exactly the type of publicity you'd want for your business. We'll try to keep a tight lid on the fact that it's your image."

"Thank you. I appreciate you trying to protect my privacy. No one wants to hire a photographer who's linked to a serial killer."

"No problem. I'll touch base with you in the morning about the security setup and when to expect the installation. The FBI team will arrive soon, but if you end up needing me tonight, let me know. Now that we know the killer has developed a special interest in you, I don't want you to be alone."

"Don't worry. My friends will be here, and I've also got my Glock."

"That's good."

"And, Rex? Make no mistake about it. If that man comes into my house again, I will use it."

Hours later, as she stared at her laptop screen, she felt anxious to hear the results of the analysis the FBI had performed earlier on her computer. Lily felt confident that the only picture taken from her darkroom was the one that had been shown on TV. What she felt far less confident about was whether anything had been taken from her computer. It would've been fairly simple to transfer pictures from her desktop. She no longer kept highly encrypted classified files, so she hadn't been particularly focused on the security of her computer.

And unlike some of her former counterparts at the CIA, technology wasn't her specialty. Tradecraft and human intelligence were her strengths. When she needed tech help, she called on others. So for now, she would have to wait for the FBI results to come in.

She walked over to the sink, and Grace nuzzled her hand while she finished up the dishes. Her pup could no doubt sense that she was feeling down about the whole situation. Though Alison and Jackson were supposed to come over, she had decided that she didn't feel like company. So she'd told them that she would be fine for the night. And she could take care of herself. Rex's concern was perfectly normal, but he assumed that he was dealing with an average citizen. Not a highly trained CIA operative.

Grace whined. "Okay, girl. This is your last time going out this evening." Thankfully, she had a large fenced-in backyard that Grace loved. Lily let her out the back door and then went into the living room and took a seat on the couch.

Her thoughts returned to her CIA past. When the truth had come out to everyone at the Agency that James had been a double agent, it should've made her feel less guilty over what had happened on the mission. But she had loved him and his deception still stung.

She closed her eyes and for a moment thought about praying. But what good would that do? She and God weren't exactly on good terms anymore. No doubt she'd made bad choices, and she had to live with those repercussions. Still, she blamed God for what had happened to her. How it had all played out and how she'd had to end things.

A loud crashing sound broke through her thoughts. Shards of glass from the window sprayed her body. Instinctively, she dropped to the ground and covered her head. Grace barked loudly from the backyard, but Lily was so thankful that she wasn't inside right now.

She bear-crawled toward the kitchen, trying to avoid as much glass as possible. But there were pieces all over the living room floor. She felt a shard cut into her arm, but she didn't stop until she reached the kitchen.

Grabbing her Glock from the kitchen drawer, she saw that her hand was covered in blood. She turned, her gun trained on a possible assailant, but she didn't see anyone. She looked out the window to the backyard, where Grace was still barking.

Slowly, she proceeded back to the living room, gun drawn. This was the second time someone had invaded her home. That was a threat she didn't take lightly.

The living room was covered with bits of glass from the broken window. Looking around, she saw the large brick that had been hurled through the glass. Was this guy trying to intimidate her? Scare her? Little did he know who he was dealing with. It wasn't likely that one of her CIA enemies would do something like this. They'd just come after her directly with an assassin's bullet. No, this felt like something else.

She grabbed her phone from the kitchen and dialed Rex.

"Lily, what is it?" he answered.

"Someone just threw a large brick through my living room window. There is glass everywhere."

"Are you okay?" he asked, his voice ragged.

"Just a few cuts. I don't think they're too deep." She looked down and saw that there was a good bit of blood though the cuts were only superficial. "Thankfully, Grace was in the backyard when it happened."

"I'm calling this in right now. Do not hang up."

Seconds later, he returned to the line. "APD is less than five minutes away. I'm also on my way over. Are your friends with you?"

"That didn't end up working out."

"You should've called me, Lily. I didn't want you alone tonight. I told you it was too dangerous. You're not taking this threat seriously enough."

She didn't respond, because she couldn't say anything at this point to make him happy.

"Stay on the line with me until APD gets there. I need to know that you are safe."

"I'm right here." She waited only a few minutes until Rex arrived at her place, along with an APD squad car.

He walked into her house and immediately started checking her over. "Are you sure you're all right? Do you need medical attention?"

"I'll be fine. It's really nothing too serious." She held out her arms to show him. "The cuts aren't that deep. Just a little blood."

He frowned and walked over to the officers who were starting to work the scene in her living room. Now that the police were in the house, she took the opportunity to get Grace safely back inside and put her into her bedroom away from the glass. She walked back down the stairs and into the kitchen, where Rex was waiting for her.

"They're gathering evidence," he said.

"It happened so quickly. What's the connection here? Why would the killer do this to me?"

"Because he's determined to finish the job he started, and extend his sick game along the way. You've proved to be a special challenge for him, and it's one that he seems to have fully embraced."

A chill shot down her arm. "That's disturbing."

"And, unfortunately, I have some more bad news."

"What?" She was almost afraid to ask.

"We've got a report of a missing graduate student."

"Oh, no."

"She fits the victim profile perfectly," he said quietly.

"You think he's already struck again? He's escalating quickly."

"I'm thinking the worst-case scenario. We have search teams looking for her. I think this guy wants us to find his victims because that's all part of the fun for him."

Her phone chirped, announcing a text. She glanced at the screen but didn't recognize the sender. It was a blank text with an attachment. Something told her that this was wrong. Still, she had to look. She opened up the attachment.

"Lily, what is it?" He took a step toward her.

Her heart thumped loudly in her chest. She looked

down at the phone and saw the photo that had been on the news. But now it was marked with a bright red X. "Rex, you should look at this." She handed him her phone. "I think I have the location for your latest victim."

THREE

Lily went with Rex to the crime scene at Westlake Park while Jackson and Guy were busy at the house boarding up her living room window. Minutes after she received the text, Rex had contacted APD to check out Westlake Park. And unfortunately, her suspicion about the next victim had been right. Rex wasn't crazy about the idea of her going to the crime scene, but she'd insisted and Rex didn't feel safe leaving her with anyone else, so he had obtained approval for her to visit the scene. She wanted to be able to help in any way she could.

In the field, she'd seen some pretty heinous things. But nothing could've really prepared her for this crime scene. This killer was truly a psychopath. And the damage he'd inflicted on this innocent woman now lying lifeless in front of her was unthinkable.

She tried to push away the emotions bubbling up below the surface and focus on how she could be of help in catching this guy. Thankfully, due to her CIA training, she was able to compartmentalize her emotions.

Rex walked over to her. "The crime scene techs don't think she was murdered in the park. Just that this is where he dumped her body. But you need to come over here and take a look behind these bushes."

Following Rex, Lily prepared herself for what she was going to see. The victim's body had been found on the jogging trail so this had to be something else that lurked behind the bushes. She took a deep breath as he shone his flashlight. And that was when she saw it. Another photo. This time it was in color, and she recognized it as a picture she'd taken of a farmhouse about twenty minutes outside the city.

"I'm assuming this is your photograph?" Rex asked.

"Yes. But I don't get this, Rex. Why would he lead us to the location through pictures? Now that we know what he's doing, why wouldn't we just get an FBI team to stake out the farmhouse and catch him when he goes there? I know exactly where it is."

Rex shook his head. "Because that's not how this guy is going to operate. He did this once—using the picture as a means to tell us where the victim was. But he isn't stupid. He'll come up with another game. I just don't know what that is yet. What is clear to me is that he's formed a very unhealthy connection to you through all of this. The killer doesn't like missteps or failures. He can't let it go."

"Yes, I understand."

He reached out and touched her arm. "This all comes back to you, Lily. He's not going to let up, and unfortunately he's got you front and center."

"That's a place I do not want to be." She was used

to being in the crosshairs but in a totally different type of deadly game. In this situation, she currently felt a severe lack of control, and that bothered her. She liked being in charge, not just sitting back and waiting for something bad to happen.

"I'm sorry you were put in this situation. But we need to talk about your personal security."

That was the last thing she wanted to talk about. She didn't want APD or the FBI providing her with protection. She could handle it herself. Especially since she knew she was a target. This wasn't a covert operation. This was an in-your-face threat. He was killing women and using her as a pawn in his game. She wasn't going to stand idly by and let him continue to use her.

"It's okay if you don't want to talk about it now, but we will need to at some point," he said. "We can't presume to understand how the mind of a sociopath like this operates."

She nodded. This man was trying to protect her. He was doing his job. It was just difficult for her to relinquish control. To trust someone. To provide full disclosure. After all, her life in the CIA had been all about withholding information. Her instincts told her that he was one of the good guys, but look how wrong she had been about James. How could she ever learn to trust again?

He gently took her arm and guided her away from the scene and back toward his SUV.

On the drive to her house, they rode in silence for

a few minutes until he spoke. "You're from Atlanta, right?" he asked.

"Yeah. It was just me and my mom growing up. Times were tough, as you can imagine. She worked two jobs just to put food on the table. The house that I live in was my grandmother's. It was the only thing of value we had."

"Where is your mom now?"

"She died my freshman year of college. She had a lot of issues and got mixed up with the wrong guys. It led to her making bad decisions. But enough of my family drama. What about you?"

"I was born and raised in Georgia. My parents are still together. Not to say there weren't some really rough patches. But they're both really solid in their faith and decided to stick it out through the good and the bad."

Interesting, she thought. "And do you share their beliefs?"

"Yes. My faith is really important to me. Especially in my line of work. Sometimes God is all I have. He's the only one I can talk to about the awful things I experience."

Her heart hurt listening to him because there was a time when she'd felt the same way. Then everything had changed. God had taken everything away from her. And she still didn't know why.

"What about you?" he asked.

"That's a long story for another time."

"I get it." He pulled up in her driveway, and she was relieved that he wasn't pushing the topic right now.

She stepped out of the SUV and walked up her front porch steps. Guy's car was in the driveway. The living room window was boarded up. Grace started barking. "She knows we're home. It looks as if the guys are still here," she said.

"Good," he said. "If the killer is watching, it's good for him to know that you have a tight circle of friends. And you're about to have the FBI protecting you, as well."

They walked into the house and Grace greeted them warmly. They found Jackson and Guy sitting in the living room. The two of them were polar opposites. Jackson was tall with dark hair and eyes, while Guy was shorter with blond hair and blue eyes. But the one thing they had in common was their loyalty to her. She'd known Guy since eighth grade when he'd moved into town. He was a good man who was currently working his way through school to be an EMT.

"Thank you both for what you did with the window."

"You're not safe here by yourself, Lily," Jackson said. He was always very protective of her. Like the big brother she never had.

"I'm glad you're concerned," Rex said. "We are, too, and will be providing Lily with FBI protection."

"Will you be taking the lead?" Jackson asked.

"If I have it my way, then yes. There are a lot of moving parts, but Lily's security is my priority."

"Well, I'm glad she won't be left alone again for some psycho to attack her," Guy said, his blue eyes bright with frustration.

"You two should get home," Lily said. "I've already taken too much time out of your night."

"We're here for you if you need us," Jackson said.

"Jackson's right, Lily. Whatever you need," Guy added.

She followed them to the door and gave them both hugs. She was fortunate to have them in her life right now.

Grace barked and Lily leaned down and gave her some rubs. "I know, girl. There's a lot going on around here right now. But everything's going to be okay."

"Come on into the kitchen." She motioned for Rex to take a seat at the kitchen table. "Would you like something to drink? I could make coffee."

"To be honest, coffee sounds amazing right now. I can't see sleep in my future anytime soon."

She took the coffee out of the cabinet and put on a pot before sitting down across from him. "I've been thinking about the farmhouse photo."

"What about it?"

"I wasn't alone the day I went out there. Alison came with me."

"What else do you remember about that day? Anything at all, even if it seems like a minute detail, could be important."

Her head started to pound and the coffee couldn't brew fast enough. "Just that Alison tagged along. We thought it would be fun and we actually brought Grace, too, and made an afternoon of it. After we got done there, Alison went home so she could get ready for a client meeting and Grace and I went to the dog park."

"Do you remember talking to anyone at the dog park? Or did you notice anyone on the periphery, watching you play with Grace?" Rex asked, his brows drawn together.

Racking her brain for useful details but coming up empty, she sighed. "No. Nothing stands out in my memory."

"A killer fitting this profile would like to terrorize. He's probably been watching you for a while. He has to handpick his victims and make sure they fit his list of characteristics."

Lily reached down for Grace, who licked her hand. "We've got to stop this guy. I don't like being attacked in my own home."

"If only it were that simple."

She stood up and got two large mugs out of the cabinet. "How do you like your coffee?"

"Just sugar, if you have it."

She poured them both a cup and put his in front of him along with the sugar and a spoon. She drank hers black. "We have to outmaneuver him. Figure out what his next move would be. Isn't that what guys like you at the FBI do?"

"It is, but like I said, we only have so much to work with. We've got video surveillance set up here now, but he has to know that. He probably won't be so bold as to come back to your house. He knows we're watching."

She took a big sip of coffee, letting the warmth flow through her. "You're giving him a lot of credit."

"Serial killers are often highly intelligent. Never underestimate the enemy, Lily. I know this is a totally different world for you."

Actually, he had no idea who she really was or what she was capable of. But her CIA past had nothing to do with the serial killer, and thinking about it brought her down. It was a dark hole that threatened to consume her if she let it. It was better to face this issue as Lily Parker, photographer, rather than Lily Parker, CIA operative. "I'm not underestimating, but I think we have to try to get out ahead of him."

He crossed his arms. "I'm sorry, but I just have to say something."

"All right." She eyed him warily.

"Something is off with you."

She raised an eyebrow. "Excuse me? Maybe it's the fact that I was attacked in my home and then someone threw a brick through my window."

"But that's just it. You've been through some terribly traumatic events, but you don't act like how I would think someone in your position should act under the circumstances."

She laughed. "And how exactly is that? What am I doing wrong?"

"It's not that you're doing anything wrong, but like I said before, you're holding back on me. The guns, the strategies, your reaction. You need to tell me what it is that I don't know. Because even if you think it has nothing to do with the attacks, you could be wrong."

"Believe me, I'm not withholding anything from you that could be helpful for the investigation."

"Which means you are withholding something."

"Don't we all have secrets in our past?"

He didn't respond immediately. "Yes, but some secrets are much more dangerous than others. I did a little digging on you. You haven't lived in Atlanta your whole life."

"No. I went away for college and then worked a few years in Virginia before coming back home. There's nothing wrong with that."

"And what kind of work did you do after you graduated college?"

It was time to try to deflect. "What does this have to do with the case?"

"It's not meant to be a trick question."

"I didn't say it was."

He frowned. "But you still haven't answered the question."

This guy was FBI. If he put in the right calls and pulled a few strings her past would be revealed. When she'd been working for the CIA, her cover was as a state department employee. Even if that was all he found out, he'd have questions about any government work she may have done. If he was persistent enough, he'd discover the truth one way or the other. The question was whether she wanted him to hear it from her or get the Agency's version of events.

He didn't break eye contact with her. "Because what if there's a missing piece of your past that somehow relates to the killer or potential future victims?"

"It's just not so cut-and-dried."

He leaned forward in his seat. "Lily, if you were doing something that might not have been on the proper side of the law, then it's even more important that you come clean. I'm not asking any of these questions to get you in trouble. I'm only trying to protect you and other potential targets out there."

She fought to keep any reaction from her face. "It's not illegal. I can promise you that."

"Well, if it's not illegal, then why can't you just tell me so we can move forward?" He took a breath. "Is it a profession that you're embarrassed of?"

She hesitated for a moment, and he latched on to it, mistakenly thinking that he'd stumbled onto something.

"Believe me, Lily, there's no shame in working odd jobs to make ends meet after college."

"I think I've led you down a completely wrong path here." What should she do?

"You need to come clean with me, Lily. Please."

It was the *please* that got her, along with his sincere brown eyes. She took a deep breath. He was right. If there was even a small chance that there was a CIA connection to all of this, she had to tell him. Lives were literally on the line. "Are you really sure you need to know?"

He nodded. "Yes, I really need to know everything you can tell me."

"Okay, then. There's a reason I didn't want the news to put out a story connecting me to the killer.

I don't want anyone to know I live here and what I do now."

"Why?"

"Because I used to work for the CIA."

Rex must be delusional because he thought that Lily had just said something that wasn't possible. "Say that again?"

"The Central Intelligence Agency. I'm sure you're very familiar with it."

He had known some things about her didn't add up, but being a spy wasn't exactly what he had in mind. Or maybe she wasn't a spy. Maybe she'd had a desk job. "And what did you do for the CIA?"

Her blue eyes were bright as she fixed her gaze on him. "My missions were classified. As a special agent with the FBI, I'm sure you can very well appreciate the sensitivity here. But I worked in the field."

"How could you not think your career as a CIA agent was relevant to this investigation?"

"The guy clearly isn't going after me because of my CIA background. My CIA life is over. It's been over."

"I didn't say that the killer was someone in the CIA, but that expands the circle of connections you have in a unique way that we have to consider. How long have you been out?"

"Nine months."

"That's not that long, Lily. Why did you leave?"

"I've already said enough for now. I really don't want to talk about the past anymore. I want to figure out how to catch this guy. If we can leverage my skills to do it, then I'm all for it. But what I'm not going to do is give you a play-by-play of my career at the CIA, not to mention the fact that I can't."

Lily was hiding even more than he had imagined. And he noticed something else. For the first time he saw pain in her eyes. Something bad had happened to her while she was at the CIA, and she didn't want to talk about it or perhaps couldn't. "Can you at least tell me what geographic regions of the world you worked?"

"Primarily Europe. I'm fluent in both French and German."

He was impressed. This woman was not only smart, beautiful and tenacious—she was dangerous. He'd heard many stories about field operatives with the CIA. They were tough and even deadly when they had to be. "We can't rule out that the killer is some-how connected to someone you knew while at the CIA, or that there's a possible link between someone in your CIA past and the other victims."

"Do you realize how many people I came into con-tact with at the Agency? That would be quite an ex-pansive list spanning the entire world. I realize you want to be thorough, but I doubt that anyone I dealt with knows any of the victims." She let out a breath.

"You're probably right about that point, but we can't discount the possibility that there could be a common link between the victims. So I'm still going to need names of people you associated with."

"All right. I'll make a list."

"And you aren't going to like my next question, either, but I have to ask it."

"Go ahead."

"Are you currently seeing anyone?"

"You mean like a boyfriend?"

"Yes," he replied.

She looked down at her coffee cup. "No. There's no one."

"What about your exes? I'll need to run them down, starting with the most recent."

"The list is pretty short."

"Still, I'll need it."

"Well, there's only been one boyfriend of any significance."

He nodded. "And what's his name?"

"James Dexter." She stood up, poured more coffee and handed him back his cup.

"I'll run him down just to make sure he's in the clear and isn't connected in any way to the other victims."

"I'm afraid that's not going to be possible."

"Why not?"

"He's dead," she said quietly.

He wasn't expecting that answer. He reached out and touched her hand. "I'm so sorry, Lily. What happened?"

Lily looked up at him as a single tear fell down her cheek. "I killed him."

FOUR

"Did you just say that you killed him? As in literally?" Rex looked into the big blue eyes of the woman in front of him. And even though she said she'd worked for the CIA, she definitely didn't seem like a cold-blooded killer to him.

"I had no choice but to take action against James," she said, barely audible.

"Tell me what happened." His heart pounded as he waited to hear her explain.

"It's a long story." She looked away and then took a sip of coffee. She wiped the single large tear from her cheek, and thankfully, no more tears fell.

It killed him to watch a woman cry. He hated to push her to talk, but he had to explore every avenue when it came to his investigation. "I've got the time. I think I need to hear this."

She nodded. "On my last mission with the Agency, I found out that James was working both sides. Basically, a double agent."

This was only getting worse. He couldn't help but

feel sorry for her. She'd obviously gone through a lot. "So James was a traitor."

"Exactly. And if you would've asked me to pick out someone on our team who was capable of selling this country out, he would've been the last one on my list. He was always so loyal, or so I thought. A real team player who would go the extra mile to help anyone who needed it. Now I can see that his attentiveness was really just opportunism, which allowed him to gain information that he could exchange for money."

"That's the way people like that work, Lily. They are master manipulators. That's how they can get away with it for so long. The FBI also has its fair share of traitors. It makes me sick."

"Well, imagine how it made me feel," she said in a raspy voice. "This was my boyfriend. Someone I thought I was potentially going to marry. The man I saw myself spending my entire life with. I don't think I have to spell out how much that hurt me."

"What did the Agency think about your relationship?"

She shrugged. "We tried to keep it quiet. But I think they knew and didn't care. There are a lot of romantic relationships that occur within the CIA, especially among field agents. We were both highly effective operatives. The most important thing from the Agency's perspective was that we were getting the job done. We both had stellar reviews and were climbing up the ladder. There was even talk about one of us being promoted to the third in command at one of the embassy hot spots. Which would've been a feat for someone our age. James was only two years older than me."

"So what happened on this last mission?"

"James wasn't even supposed to be there. Not from the CIA side anyway. I was working by myself. I can't go into the operational details of the mission because that's still classified."

"I understand."

"But I was meeting with one of my assets, and James showed up. He killed the person right there on the spot before I could get the critical information that I needed from them. It was in that moment that I knew he was working both sides. The realization hit me like a sledgehammer. I'll never forget that exact moment as long as I live. Talk about life changing."

"So you killed him in self-defense," he said softly.

She nodded. "I could say it's the hardest thing I've ever done, but honestly in that moment it was a pure survival reflex. I knew he was about to pull the trigger. He'd just killed my asset, and then he turned and pointed the gun at me. So I did the only thing I could do. I got the shot off before he could shoot me first."

He reached out and grabbed her hand. "Lily, no one should have to go through something like that."

"It was the lowest point of my life. Then I had to go back to the Agency and explain the entire situation. Literally over and over again. I was polygraphed three times by three different examiners. I was put on leave during the internal investigation. All of James's subterfuge came out, but it was a long and difficult process. And because of our relationship and the way things ended, I was also considered a security risk. So they had to make absolutely sure that I wasn't a double agent, too."

"I'm so sorry."

"At the end of the day, my name was completely cleared. But the damage was already done as far as I was concerned. I never went back to work, even after they told me I could. I left the Agency and moved here to my hometown. Started my photography business. A totally new and fresh start doing something radically different."

He had never met anyone like Lily before. Most people would've crumbled under the pressure and stress of such an ordeal, but she'd chosen to go after another dream instead. "That was a very brave move."

She laughed. "Some would call it more cowardly than brave. I did run away from my troubles. Instead of continuing with my CIA career, I just cut my losses and left it all."

"No, you made the best decision you could make for yourself at the time. You had to deal with James's betrayal, not only as a CIA agent but also on a personal level. Those things don't just resolve themselves easily. No one could question your motives for leaving."

"It sounds as if you speak from experience."

"Well, it was nothing like what you went through, but I have been betrayed before by someone I cared for." He paused. This wasn't the time to talk about the problems of his past. He wanted to focus on her. "But enough about me. I appreciate you telling me all of this. I know it wasn't easy, but now I have a better understanding of your background and all you've dealt with as you transitioned from the Agency to your new life here in Atlanta."

She reached out and put her hand on his shoulder. "And now you can see why I don't want to be in the news. There are people who would want to harm me if they knew I was an easy target sitting here in Atlanta."

"You mean foreign agents?"

"Yes. I made a lot of friends while on the inside, but I made my share of enemies, too. It's all part of the job. Also, it's possible that the people James worked for would try to come after me if they knew where I lived. I'm not even sure exactly who he reported to. Just that it was a foreign government."

"Which one?"

"I can't say. And honestly, I'm not even a hundred percent certain myself, although I do have my theories."

He was frustrated by all of the security clearance issues, but he understood protocol.

"I just don't want any extra attention put on me," she said. "It's always best for former operatives to live a low-profile life, at least for a few years. Put some time in between themselves and the missions. Even if this weren't happening, I'd still want to lie low. It's one of the reasons I chose photography—in addition to really enjoying it."

"I totally agree. There's enough of a threat against you already without adding enemies from your CIA past. Even if the chance of any of them finding you and acting on it is small, there's no reason to risk it unnecessarily."

"I used many different aliases over the years. But I didn't radically change my appearance for most jobs. That's why I'm trying to keep my actual photo out of the news."

"I'll do my best. You know how reporters are, but we'll try to prevent any leaks."

"And you can see why I don't think this killer has anything to do with my time at the Agency. If one of my enemies wanted me dead, they'd shoot to kill. Put a hit out on me. End of story. This dramatic game of cat and mouse is something very different. It's not tradecraft, I can tell you that much."

"I would tend to agree with you." He finished up his coffee and set down the empty cup. "What about your past before the CIA? Boyfriends from high school or college? Even if they weren't as serious as James, I'd like to be able to run them down, too, and check their connections to the other victims."

Her cheeks flushed pink, and she shook her head. "It's kind of embarrassing, but I was what you would call a late bloomer. I didn't really date at all. I was so focused on school, and then after college I went straight to the CIA."

"There's nothing wrong with that," he said.

"How do you think the killer found me?"

"It would be all speculation at this point. But it could've been something as simple as him seeing you out and about in your daily life. He targeted you because you met his checklist of qualifications. Once he'd honed in on his type and decided to kill women who fit his profile, there was nothing you could do."

"But then he tried to kill me and failed."

"Exactly. Which made this personal for him. He didn't like being foiled by a woman. Lily, now you're a special target to him because he can't have a loose end, and he definitely can't have failure. He's probably a perfectionist with OCD tendencies. All of those characteristics get amplified in the mind of a serial killer to become a lethal combination."

Her eyes narrowed. "We'll catch him."

"I don't know if I like the sound of *we*. The FBI's priority is to catch this guy, and right now my priority is to keep you safe. You aren't actually responsible for finding him."

"I appreciate that. But we can't pretend that I'm a regular victim here. I think it helps that I have a lot of experience keeping myself safe." She smiled for the first time since this conversation started. He couldn't help but smile, too.

"Tell me more about your friends."

"Alison Cruz and I have known each other since second grade. She's my best friend. She has an interior design business and has an amazing eye for decorating. I met Jackson Bray in sixth grade and Guy Randolph in eighth grade."

"What do the guys do for a living?"

"Jackson works in marketing for a technology company, and Guy is going to school to be an EMT. The four of us were a very close-knit group. We all kind of went our separate ways for college or jobs. Alison and Jackson left Atlanta to go to school in Athens at the University of Georgia. But they moved back after graduation. When I came back it was as if we all picked up where we left off."

"I'd like to talk to them individually."

"I'm sure they'll help in any way they can. You could probably tell that the guys are very protective of me."

Grace barked and he looked down at his watch. "It's getting late, but I'm not leaving you alone. I know we haven't discussed all the logistics, but as far as I'm concerned, you need 24/7 protective detail. Even if it's not likely that the killer would come back to your house, I'm not willing to take that type of risk. The downside is just too high."

"I'm not saying I like it, but I get where you're coming from. I have a guest room down here on the first floor across from my darkroom that you or anyone else from your team is welcome to use."

"Thank you, Lily. Get some rest. Nothing is going to happen to you on my watch." And he was dead serious about that.

The next morning Lily couldn't believe she had opened up to Rex about what had happened with James. She hadn't told anyone about it other than the people she had to talk to at the Agency, including the psychologist she'd been ordered to visit. That session had been particularly painful. Mainly because she had absolutely zero interest in opening up to the person sitting in the chair, trying to get inside her head. Trying to break her down before the Agency was going to attempt to put her back together.

She headed downstairs with Grace, ready to take her for a walk. Rex was sitting at her kitchen table drinking coffee.

"Good morning," he said. "How did you sleep?"

"Considering everything going on, I think I slept pretty decent. I need to take Grace on a walk."

He stood up from the kitchen chair. "You know I'm coming with you."

"I figured you'd say that."

The doorbell rang and Grace started barking. "It's okay, Grace." She started walking toward the door and Rex grabbed her arm.

"Let me see who that is," he said.

She could already tell she wasn't going to adjust well to her new bodyguard. She was so accustomed to fighting her own battles. Taking care of herself. Watching her own back. It felt strange to have someone there doing that for her.

But, as directed, she remained standing in the kitchen while Rex went to the door. She heard male voices.

Derrick and Sean walked in with Rex. Both men were tall and presented themselves with confidence. She surmised that Sean was a few years younger than Derrick and fairly new to the job. He wore his brown hair cut shorter than Derrick's.

"Hey, guys," she said.

"We're sorry about all of this," Derrick said. He reached down and gave Grace a hearty pat on the rump.

"It's not your fault that there's a killer out there."

"Not just any killer," Sean said. "A serial killer with your name on his hit list." His brown eyes didn't show any sign of levity.

"Yeah, we were talking about that just last night," Rex added.

"What brings you to the house?" she asked.

"We wanted to regroup with Rex. The FBI is gathering additional resources to assist in the investigation, since Rex volunteered to take over your security in addition to working the case."

"Have there been any new developments since last night?" she asked.

"Thankfully, no," Derrick said. "We don't know how long this guy's cooling-off period is going to be. But there's a high likelihood that he will contact you again. Also, have you thought about what the photo he left at the last scene could mean? The one of the farmhouse?" Derrick asked.

"I thought about it a lot while I was trying to fall asleep last night, and I have no idea what he's trying to say with that picture. There's no special significance that I can think of."

"To you, maybe," Rex said. "But in the mind of a serial killer it could have meant something."

"Sorry to interrupt this discussion, guys, but I really need to walk Grace." Her sweet dog was waiting patiently, but she knew that Grace would need to go.

"Of course," Derrick said. "We'll wait here until you folks get back."

She leashed Grace up and walked out the front door with Rex right by her side. He was in full FBI alert mode. She didn't really think that she was in danger in broad daylight in the middle of her neighborhood. But it was Rex's job to be cautious and she appreciated that.

They were only about halfway down the street when they saw Alison and Jackson approaching them. "They were probably coming over to the house to check on me. Alison lives just down the block and Jackson is only an additional block away."

Grace excitedly tugged on her leash to greet them as they quickly approached.

"We were worried about you," Alison said. "I heard all about Jackson and Guy boarding up your window after it was smashed in. That's horrific. You could've really been hurt, Lily."

"I'm fine though, Alison. Just a few cuts from making my way through the glass. And, thankfully, Grace was outside."

"We saw on the news that they are no closer to catching this guy." Jackson frowned. "Or at least that's what they're reporting. The media is having a field day with this. Saying that this guy could turn out to be the deadliest killer that Atlanta has ever seen. Is that true?"

"I'm not going to attempt to minimize the threat here. We're adding more FBI resources, plus we have Atlanta police working the case, too," Rex said.

"Bringing the killer to justice is a top priority for FBI and local law enforcement."

Alison reached out and touched her arm. "And what about you, Lily? What are you going to do?"

"I'm going to keep on living my life and trying to help with this case any way I can." Grace tugged and Lily continued walking with her friends and Rex.

"And I'm going to be by her side," Rex said. "We're not going to leave her without protection. We understand the stakes here."

"You think you can keep Lily safe?" Alison asked.

Lily could see the worry and apprehension in her friend's dark eyes.

"Absolutely," Rex replied. "Lily's safety is my priority."

"We'll do anything we can to help, too," Alison said. "I just can't fathom that anyone would want to hurt Lily. Much less kill all those innocent women. It's so scary."

"Guys like this can't stay under the radar forever," Lily said. "He'll get overconfident and make a mistake. And law enforcement will be there when he does."

"I hope so," Jackson said. "Because we can't have anything happen to you." Reaching out, he put his arm around her and gave her shoulder a squeeze. "And you know I have my new cabin about half an hour from here. You are welcome to stay there if you want a safe place outside the city."

"Thank you, but right now I'm staying put."

She was fortunate to have such friends in her

life. Then she remembered there was something she wanted to ask. "Oh, Alison," Lily said. "Do you remember anything special about that day you and I went to the farmhouse and I took photos?"

"No. It was just like any other outing. I remember you saying you got some great shots. Why?"

"Because the killer left a photo of the farmhouse at the latest crime scene."

Alison pulled in a deep breath. "Lily, this is all too much." Alison turned toward Rex and grabbed his arm. "Shouldn't you take her away somewhere safe? Somewhere this psychopath can't get to her?"

Before Rex could say anything, Lily jumped in. "I can't just run away," she said. "If I did, he might just redirect his attention to some innocent, unsuspecting victim. We know this guy has an issue with me because I stood up to him. We can beat him at his own game."

"Lily's right," Rex said. "At least at this point. Depending on how this guy reacts, the threat assessment may change in the future. But like I said, Lily won't be left alone under any circumstances." Rex turned his attention to her friends. "Could I talk to the two of you before you go? I'd like to just make sure I rule out any possible connections between anyone you know and our other victims."

"Sure," Alison and Jackson said in unison.

"Let's head back to the house and you can talk to Rex there." Lily was certain of one thing. She wasn't going to run away. She was going to face this madman down. He'd messed with the wrong girl.

* * *

Rex looked over at the petite, long-haired brunette sitting across from him at the table. Alison's big, deep-chocolate eyes showed her sincere concern for her best friend. It tugged at his gut to see this woman in pain and worry, but he had a job to do.

"Would you like a soda or water or anything before we get started?"

Alison shook her head. "No, I'm good. I just want to be able to help Lily. To be able to do something to stop all of this."

"I understand. Why don't we back up a bit before we jump into things. You and Lily have known each other since you were little, correct?" Rex was going to use this opportunity to find out more about Lily's past. Even if it was more for his own benefit than the investigation itself.

Alison smiled. "Yes. We were inseparable growing up. Lily spent a lot of time at my house. My late mother, God bless her soul, acted like a second mother to Lily. Her mom's intentions were good, but she had a really bad follow-through. Got mixed up in drugs and that lifestyle. It was bad, so Lily spent nights at my house a lot. I'm so thankful we were able to be here for her. If you haven't figured it out yet, Lily is fiercely independent. I think what happened with her mom is one of the reasons she's like that."

"Yeah, I've gotten the impression that even growing up Lily was a bit of a loner. Only relying on her small group of friends."

"I hate that she has to go through this," Alison

said. "Lily has the kindest heart. For her it's all about Grace and her photography. As a business owner myself, I can totally sympathize. It takes a lot of work to get a business up and running. And then keep it up."

He waited a few more minutes to see if he was missing something, but as much as Alison wanted to help, none of her information was particularly helpful. He'd cross-referenced the list of names from the friends and acquaintances of the other victims with hers and had come up empty.

"Thanks for your help, Alison. Can you tell Jackson I'm ready to talk to him now?"

"Sure." Alison reached out and grabbed on to his hands. "Please protect Lily. I know she seems so strong on the outside, but she still needs someone watching her back."

"Of course. You have my word that I will do everything in my power to keep her safe."

"Good." Alison stood up and walked out of the room.

A minute later, Jackson walked in. Lily's tall, dark-haired friend shared Alison's concern. He took a seat without saying a word.

"I know you're worried about Lily and you have every right to be."

"Lily is one of my closest friends on this earth. I can't fathom something bad happening to her."

"That's why I wanted to talk to you. To see if you have any connections to the other victims. And, of course, to find out if you have any additional input that may be useful to the investigation."

"Have you considered the fact that the killer could've found Lily through her job? She's had a lot of male clients through her photography business."

Rex made a note to double-check Lily's client list again. They'd done one review, but Jackson made a valid point. "Is there anyone in particular you can think of?"

"No, but even beyond her clients, she's done a number of weddings. I imagine she'd get attention from some of the male guests in attendance."

Jackson was right. The web of possibilities was beginning to seem endless.

Rex turned his full attention back to Jackson. "You clearly care about Lily. Is there anything else you think I should know? Anything, no matter how small, that you think might provide a fuller picture?"

"If I had information, believe me, I'd give it to you. Lily isn't the type of woman that people want to hurt. She's difficult to get to know, but once you do, you see how sweet her heart is. I can't imagine someone wanting her dead. It boggles my mind."

"I appreciate you taking the time to talk."

"Happy to help. The only other thing I wanted to mention is that I'm concerned about Lily staying in this house, and again I'll offer up my cabin if you need it."

"Thank you for the offer, but we're good here. The house is under police and FBI protection. I can assure you of that."

"But we know that the killer knows how to find

her. Wouldn't it be safer to move her somewhere else?"

"We're constantly evaluating options. This is not something we take lightly. And I can guarantee you that I'm not going anywhere. I'll be by her side, regardless."

Jackson's brown eyes narrowed. "Please keep her safe. Don't underestimate this guy. Please."

"You have my word." Rex realized he'd been making a lot of promises lately. He prayed he'd be able to keep them all.

Later that night, Rex stared at his laptop. Lily was in the living room watching TV, and he was in the kitchen catching up on all the FBI and APD emails related to the investigation. He was trying to put the pieces of this strange puzzle together. Unfortunately, he knew that time was never on his side in a case like this.

One fact remained indisputable. All the women were physically similar to Lily. But there didn't seem to be any other link between the victims outside that. None of the victims appeared to know each other. He'd run all types of scenarios and factual data points to try to find connections, but there simply weren't any that he'd been able to uncover yet.

Serial killers were usually very methodical. If he had already decided what his victim profile was going to be, it was unlikely this guy would start killing tall, blonde women. Serial killers were typically also highly focused on reaching their goals. Which meant that he probably wasn't going to give up on his pursuit of Lily.

He reviewed his file of notes to see if there was something he had missed. As far as the attacks on Lily went, there was the initial incident at her house and the note left at the hospital. Plus, her window being broken. But that was probably more of a warning shot than anything else. A clear signal that the killer wasn't done with her yet. Then he had communicated with her electronically via text. Rex had a sneaking suspicion that he would do that again. The perpetrator wanted to feel close to Lily.

Unlike with the other victims, the killer was trying to interact with Lily. Develop some sort of rapport with her. Yet his intention was also to intimidate her, as evidenced by the fact that he'd attacked her twice in her own home, the place she should have felt the safest. But Rex feared that when the murderer tired of that approach, his intentions toward Lily would turn deadly in a much more direct fashion. And there was absolutely no way of knowing how long he would toy with her before taking things to the next level.

Also, there was the CIA wildcard. He'd quickly called in FBI agents who held top-secret security clearances, and they'd worked with the CIA to cross-reference the names and identities of operatives Lily had worked with. While Rex didn't have the security clearance to view the names, he'd gotten the bottom-line results. There were no linkages at all between anyone that Lily worked with at the Agency and any of the other victims or their contacts. It appeared that

Lily was correct in her assessment that this killer had nothing to do with her time at the CIA.

He tapped away on his keyboard, recording all of his thoughts. Grace had been keeping him company, lying at his feet. He enjoyed the canine companionship. It also made him realize how lonely he probably was, although he'd never admit that to anyone. He could barely admit it to himself. It was easier to live in denial. To keep his guard up and his limited emotions in check.

Then, as he was pondering what file to review next, the room suddenly turned dark. Without hesitation, he jumped to his feet and made his way to the living room. He had a penlight that he always kept on him and he shone it to light his way. "Lily, are you all right?"

"Yes, I'm totally fine," she said. "Maybe it's just a power outage."

He knew better than to assume that. "You don't believe that any more than I do."

"You're right," she said."

"I need to check things out."

"I have my downstairs gun in the kitchen."

"Let me grab it for you." He jogged back into the kitchen and opened the drawer that he knew contained one of her guns. Then he walked back into the living room.

"Stay put here." He handed her the gun. "Just please don't shoot me by accident."

"Roger that," she said. "Go."

Grace started barking and Rex scoped out the

rest of the first floor. He felt confident there was no one inside. He was far less confident about what was going on outside.

He circled back around to the living room. "Lily, has anything happened here?"

"Nothing here. We're fine."

A loud crashing noise came from the back porch. "I'll be back. I need to see what's happening out there. Call Grace and keep her with you in the living room."

Lily did as she was told. He could hear the dog moving through the room.

"Do you have her?"

"Yes. We're okay, and I'm not letting her go."

"Okay. Stay alert. I'm calling in backup, but I can't wait. I need to check this out now to determine if I need to move you or if it's safer to stay here." He couldn't have anything happening to either of them. Lily might be a trained CIA operative, but he wasn't taking any chances. After quickly putting in the call for backup, he took deliberate steps toward the back porch, where he heard more noises.

He used his penlight to illuminate the porch. But it wasn't a broad enough beam to show him much more than what was directly in front of him. Another crashing noise sounded.

Slowly unlocking the door, he stepped out onto the porch. That was when he noticed the streetlights and the lights that were on in other houses. Someone had intentionally cut Lily's power. Quickly, he surveyed his surroundings. A potted plant in a ceramic container lay splattered on the porch along with two overturned chairs.

He prayed for guidance as he made a split-second decision. It was more important for him to go back inside and guard Lily. This could be a diversion attempt. Or worse.

Rex took a step back toward the door just as he felt the bullet slice through his left arm. Caught off guard and trying to avoid a second hit, he stumbled forward, fighting to stay upright, but then fell and hit his head hard on the edge of patio table. His world went dark.

FIVE

Lily heard the gunshot and then a loud thud from the porch as Grace barked even more loudly. Yeah, Rex had told her to stay put, but she wasn't just going to be huddled up on the couch like a sitting duck. Something was going down on the back porch, and she had no doubt that she could help Rex if he needed it.

But while she may be cavalier about herself, Grace was another matter. Not wasting another moment, she led Grace down to the guest room where Rex was staying and closed her in there. Then she quickly made her way to the porch. Even in the dark, she knew her way around her own home very well.

It was actually lighter outside than inside because of the moonlight. She tried to open the porch door but was met with some resistance. She pushed on the door once again, and that was when she saw him.

Rex was on the ground, his body partially blocking the door. Her heart pounding, she nudged him. He wasn't responsive. She didn't want to move him without knowing how badly he was injured, but she had no choice. So she pushed open the door to be able to get out, which shifted his body slightly on the ground.

Once outside, she crouched down beside him, checking for a pulse, and felt liquid on her hands. Blood!

Had he been shot? And where? She'd wrongly assumed that he had been the one firing his weapon. This changed everything.

She tried desperately to determine where the bleeding was coming from, but in the moonlight she could only do so much. She wasn't concerned for her own safety, but she was worried about the shooter still being out there and getting another shot off that would hit Rex.

She caught herself almost praying for Rex but realized that wouldn't do a bit of good. Not coming from her.

Instead, she focused on what she could do as she tried her best to stabilize Rex in his unknown condition. Even though she was very strong for her size, she didn't know if she was strong enough to move an unconscious man who was over six feet tall and weighed two hundred plus.

But aware that they were possibly still in danger, she had to do what she could to get him to safety. She pushed the door all the way open and then, using all of her strength, attempted to drag a totally unresponsive Rex through the doorway. After a minute, she had to stop to take a few deep breaths.

Sweat started to form on her brow and trickled down her back. This man was even heavier than he looked and made of solid muscle. But that obstacle didn't deter her from pulling his body toward door to try to protect the both of them from the shooter.

This killer hadn't just gone after her, but now he was going after the man trying his best to protect her. Seething with anger, she was even more determined to find him and put an end to his madness.

When she heard the sirens approaching, she let out a sigh of relief just as the lights flickered back on. With the benefit of the back porch light she could now clearly see that Rex had been shot in the arm. And he had a large red spot on the side of his temple.

She looked and saw Officer Sean Bishop running up the porch steps from the backyard. She sure could've used his help five minutes ago.

"Lily, are you all right?" Sean's eyes were wide with concern.

"I'm fine, but Rex isn't. Where did you come from?"

"I wasn't far away when the emergency call came in from Rex. When I got here there was no answer at the front door, so I came to the backyard to check things out. Additional backup is only a minute or two out."

"Good," she said, still trying to catch her breath.

"What happened here?" Sean asked. He knelt down beside Rex.

"We were in the house when the lights went out. Rex went outside to check on things because we heard loud crashing sounds. Then, after a minute, I heard gunshots from the porch, and I was worried something had happened to Rex. That's when I found him bleeding by the back door." She looked around at the porch. It was a mess, with overturned chairs and broken potted plants. The killer had purposely tried to make a racket to draw Rex out of the house. It was a solid plan, and if he'd been a better shot, Rex would probably be dead right now.

"Sounds as if it could've been a whole lot worse," Sean said. "And you're sure that you're all right?"

"Yes, I'm perfectly fine."

Within minutes, her house was swarming with APD officers.

She looked on with great interest as the EMT started to provide care to Rex.

"What do you know about his injuries, ma'am?" the EMT asked her.

"I think he was shot and also suffered some type of head injury. I moved him to try to get us both out of the line of fire."

"Understood," the paramedic said as he quickly went to work.

Lily stood silent for a moment as she watched the man work on Rex. Her pulse raced as she waited to hear how Rex was doing.

"The gunshot wound is actually not that bad," the EMT said. "He's probably unconscious from falling after being shot. Looks like he knocked his head pretty good, given the color and swelling. The gunshot wound is largely superficial and that is what's most important."

"That's good news," Sean said.

Lily was so glad that Rex was going to be okay. Derrick showed up and she recounted the entire story to him.

"How in the world did you move him, Lily?" Derrick asked with wide blue eyes.

"I'm stronger than I look." She couldn't help but smile. Nothing wrong with a little levity to break the tension.

"Yes, she is," Rex said.

She looked over and Rex's eyes were open. They had him laid up on a gurney and were ready to transport him to the hospital in the ambulance. A flood of relief surged through her to see that he had regained consciousness.

"Rex, what happened out here?" She rushed to his side and Derrick was right behind her. "I heard the gunshot, but I didn't realize it was you getting shot until I saw you on the ground, covered in blood."

"Yeah. So I came outside to determine what was going on, and that's when I saw the mess. All the chairs and pots overturned." He grimaced in pain. "I realized that you were vulnerable to attack, that I needed return to you. If I wouldn't have stepped backward to go inside it would've probably been a direct hit. But I stumbled and fell and hit my head. Then I blacked out. That's all I remember."

Derrick took a step toward him. "Well, now you're going to the hospital."

"No way. I'm perfectly fine," Rex said. "I just need to be bandaged up and I'm good to go."

"There's no point in arguing about this," Derrick

said. "You're getting checked out. We can't risk you having a concussion and passing out later."

"I'll come with you," Lily said to Rex. "I know you're worried about me, but we need to get you patched up and confirm that your injuries aren't serious."

"See, that's a plan. I'll bring Lily with me to the hospital," Derrick said. "We'll meet you there. Then we can determine next steps based on the prognosis from the doctor. This isn't the time to try to play hero. There's too much on the line here."

"Well, I don't like it, I think I'm fine. But I understand why you're making me go."

"Good," Lily said. "We'll meet you there." She watched as he was wheeled into the ambulance. They were fortunate. The outcome could've been much worse. The killer was proving that he had no intention of letting up. She feared next time he might actually succeed.

Rex couldn't believe he'd been shot. Even more troubling was how close he'd come to a direct hit, and that would've left Lily completely at the mercy of the killer. He'd been discharged from the hospital after a couple of hours and had gone back to Lily's place. There was no way he was leaving her with anyone else.

An APD officer had been stationed outside overnight to provide an additional layer of security. Now, after breakfast, he was looking into Lily's serious blue eyes as she sat on the living room couch.

"We need to talk," Rex said.

"What do you think about what happened last night? I'm getting to know how your mind works. You've already got a full-blown theory, don't you?"

He gave her a slight smile. They were discovering more and more about each other every day. "I think the killer was trying to take me out as a way to get to you directly. He's getting antsy playing his own game, and he won't rest until he finishes the job he started."

"That's highly troubling," she said softly.

He felt he had to put it all out there even if it was disturbing. "I realize that. I'm not saying it to try to unduly scare you, but I think the theory has merit." He paused. "Although I think I've figured out that it probably takes a lot to actually scare you."

"You're right about that, but there is something I've been meaning to ask you about. Do you think my friends are in any danger?"

"Unfortunately, I don't think it's safe for them to be spending too much time around you. The killer is watching. And while you're the primary target, we don't want them getting caught in the crosshairs."

She patted Grace, who was lying beside her. "Speaking of him watching, what happened with the FBI video surveillance of my house that you had set up?"

"I just got an email on that issue this morning from our FBI techs."

"Uh-oh. This isn't going to be good, is it?"

He shook his head. "No. In addition to being a cold-blooded killer, our guy is apparently great with technology. He was able to disable the video surveillance and turn the power off remotely."

"Is there a way we can outsmart him on the tech side?"

"We've got good people, too, but the consensus is that he'll be able to get around our systems if he sets his mind to it."

She let out a loud sigh. "This is crazy."

He reached out and put his hand on top of hers. "Don't get discouraged. Someone this bold is bound to slip up."

"Hopefully he'll make a big mistake before he kills another innocent woman."

"You're right. I'm praying that we catch him quickly."

She rolled her eyes. "Sorry, Rex. I hate to break it to you, but I don't know if prayer is really going to help. We should probably stick to tried-and-true investigation techniques."

Pain and skepticism were etched on her face. "Do you really mean that? You think prayer is worthless under these circumstances?"

"Sorry." She removed her hand from under his. "I shouldn't have insulted your faith. We need all the help we can get, but it just won't come from me trying to pray. I can promise you that much. God isn't in the business of answering my prayers."

"Anything you want to talk about?" He knew there was something more going on with her stance on faith. People didn't make comments like that for no reason.

She averted her eyes. "Not really." Her phone chirped and she picked it up from the coffee table. She didn't speak, but he watched her facial expression change as she pursed her lips.

"It's him," she said. "He sent me another text. It's from a different account but it's our guy."

"What does it say?"

She looked down at her phone and then back up and then back down again. "'Next time I won't miss.'" She handed the phone to him so he could read it for himself.

He nodded. "Just as I suspected. His fixation is growing stronger and stronger with each passing day and he won't be satisfied until he accomplishes his ultimate goal."

"We have to make sure that he never reaches that goal. We also need to stop him before he kills other women on his list."

"Agreed, but you know that's much easier said than done."

The phone chirped again. "Oh, no," she said. "What is it now?"

Since he still had her phone in his hand, he opened the second text message. Well, that was strange. He wouldn't have expected this twist. "It's a picture of you."

She took the phone back from him and examined the picture. "This is a picture of when I was leaving the hospital. See the background? You can see the hospital."

"Yes. He sent you this picture because he wants

you to know that you're still a target. I'd like to consult with one of our other serial killer experts at the Bureau to see if they can provide any more insight on how this guy's deadly plan may continue to unfold. I think we could benefit from having the expertise of someone who has dealt with serial killers longer than I have and who might have had a similar situation in the past. Meanwhile, we need to figure out what we're going to do about your security in the short term. I'd like to beef up the detail on the perimeter of the house."

"I think that would be prudent. Also, what about my friends? I know Alison and Jackson were going to come over today to visit."

He admired the fact that she was so protective of her friends. "I think it's fine today, but we need to talk to them about the risks involved with them being around you and probably suggest they lie low for a bit."

"The absolute last thing I want to do is put any of my friends in danger. I'd never forgive myself if something happened to them."

He reached out and touched her arm. "I know that. We'll get through this, Lily. I promise you that."

"Are you sure you should be making promises you don't know you can keep?"

"I intend to keep that promise."

"And what about your life? You can't just give up your life to provide protection for me around the clock. I'm sure you have friends and probably someone special in your life. What about them? I'm not worth giving all that up for. I know that much."

He shook his head. If only Lily knew how empty his life really was. "Don't ever think that you're not worth my time, Lily. You're worth it and then some."

"There's no need for you to say that."

"It's true. And beyond that, my job is my everything."

"I find it hard to believe that you don't have any personal life."

"I have a couple of close friends, including Derrick. But romantic relationships are too difficult to maintain, given my line of work." Plus, he wasn't going to bring up the fact that he'd given up his heart once and it had been trampled on. He didn't ever want to be vulnerable like that again. To feel that pain again. No, it was better to live alone.

"Well, who am I to talk about relationships? You know what happened with my last one. That was enough to make me okay with being single the rest of my life."

He laughed. "I think we have a lot in common, Lily."

"Are you going to tell the police about my CIA background?"

"Only Derrick. The rest of the police team doesn't need to know, but I wanted someone else in the loop."

She nodded in agreement. "That makes sense."

"And besides that, Derrick was pretty impressed with how you dragged me back into the house last night. I think he was starting to realize that there was something about your story that didn't add up. You're unlike any photographer we've ever met before, that's for sure."

"I'm not going to lie. Moving you was no easy task. You're even heavier than you look."

He smiled. "You're a strong woman, Lily. And not only in the physical sense. I'm sorry this is happening to you, but if it had to happen to someone, at least it's someone with your background and strengths. I fear that most people wouldn't have had the internal fortitude to make it through each day, but you've been a rock."

"Thanks, Rex."

He looked at her and couldn't help but want to know even more about this woman who continued to amaze him.

As Lily walked into the FBI field office in Atlanta, a wave of apprehension washed over her. She'd been processed by security and her visitor's badge now hung prominently around her neck.

She looked over at Rex, who was in his element. This was basically his home. From what she gathered, even on nights and weekends, he spent much more time here than he did at his house. She followed him into a conference room on the third floor.

This strategy meeting was Rex's idea, and Lily had to admit that it was a good one. Bring everyone together in one room and talk out the case. But ever since the latest text from the killer yesterday, Lily had been uneasy. And not just for the obvious reason that there was a serial killer on the loose, who also happened to be obsessed with taking her out.

No, it was much deeper than that. Something about the entire situation felt off to her, but she couldn't really explain why. It bothered her that she hadn't isolated the issue that was causing her the most concern.

Lily took a seat beside Rex at a big, dark conference room table and waited for the others to join them. Within a couple of minutes, Derrick and Sean came into the room, along with a woman she didn't recognize.

She stood up from her chair to greet them all.

"Lily," Rex said. "This is Special Agent Eliza Newton. She's one of the Bureau's most skillful agents specializing in serial killers."

The petite brunette FBI agent with big hazel eyes gave her a firm handshake. She liked the woman instantly.

"Lily," Eliza said. "I can't even begin to imagine what this has been like for you."

"I just want to catch the guy before he hurts anyone else." And that was the truth. She feared that this psychopath wasn't going to stop. Which meant that it was up to them to stop him. Lily understood that it wasn't going to be an easy job.

"Please, everyone. Take a seat so we can get started," Eliza said.

Lily proceeded to sit back down in the large conference room chair and the others followed suit.

"I thought it would be a good idea for us to get together and talk about the latest developments," Rex said. "I asked Eliza to get involved because of her extensive experience with serial killers. Were you able to read the file?"

Eliza nodded. "Yes, I'm up-to-date. The last documented item took place yesterday with a text contact from the killer to Lily. Has there been anything else since then that hasn't made its way into the file?"

"No," Rex said. "Now that we're electronic, I am doing my best to keep the database updated in real time, given the number of different messages."

"Thank you," Eliza said. "Having the real-time flow of information is really important. I also read about how the killer came after you directly, Rex. He clearly sees you as a threat in his quest to take out Lily."

"The question is what do we do about all of this?" Derrick asked. He leaned forward in his seat. "And what is this guy's next play? He's already killed five women. We don't need a sixth victim. We want to do everything in our power to try to stop this guy before he strikes again. So I'm all for any assistance you can provide. Any theory you have, no matter how far-fetched. I think we should put it all out on the table."

Eliza stood up and started to write on the whiteboard. "I agree. Let's start with the facts. Lily, the killer picked a certain type of victim. That type of victim happened to also fit your physical characteristics, age and the fact that you live alone. So after he picked his target type, he somehow came into contact with you and then determined that you would be his next victim. So he breaks into your house with the explicit intention of killing you, but you thwarted his attack. You fought back. He probably wasn't expecting you to be able to take him on, but you did. And because of that, you became the number one target in his mind. He elevated you to a special status because, as far as we know, you're the only victim he's chosen that has been able to get away."

Eliza took a deep breath and continued to write on the board. Then she turned around and addressed the group. "And from the file it appears that no one has been able to find any connection between the victims or people that the victims knew, correct?"

"You're right about that," Rex said. "It hasn't been for lack of trying, but we've come upon a lot of dead ends. What are you thinking, Eliza?"

"I'm wondering if the killer has a specific place that he likes to find his victims. Even if the victims didn't know each other, have you thought about certain places or activities that they shared as part of their routine? Maybe they all shop at the same store or go to the same hair salon?"

"You're right," Rex said. "I hadn't been focusing on that particular angle."

"Because if you get any leads there, then you have a starting point for trying to catch this guy in the act of finding his next target." Eliza let out a big breath. "But don't get your hopes up. This might be a long shot."

"At this point, we'll take any and all ideas on where you think this guy is headed with his current strategy," Rex said.

Eliza took a seat and tapped her pen quickly against her legal pad.

Rex crossed his arms. "So next steps. What's your opinion, Eliza, on Lily responding to the text from the killer?"

Eliza leaned forward in her seat. "There are different schools of thought on that. On the one hand, a direct communication from Lily could satisfy him and cause him to keep his focus on her, buying us some time to continue our investigation before he finds his next victim. But there are other experts in the field who caution against any direct contact with a serial killer. You're feeding their obsessive tendencies, possibly causing them to escalate their efforts."

"What would be your recommendation?" Lily asked.

"I would hold off on any direct contact for now. It's a calculated risk and, in my opinion, the payoff isn't as large as the potential downside. There may come a time when it makes sense, but I don't think we're at that point."

"What about Lily's personal security?" Sean asked. "Do you think we should move her to some sort of safe house?"

Eliza shook her head. "I'm actually concerned about the repercussions of that. A move at this juncture could be premature. Yes, Lily could potentially be safer, but if our killer loses connection with her, then he may go off the deep end. I realize that Lily may not be on board with that approach. It's asking a lot of someone." She directed her attention to Lily.

"I'd completely understand, Lily, if you wanted to leave. I'm sure the FBI would provide you with a totally secure safe house."

"That's exactly what I told her, too" Rex said. "Ultimately, I think Lily should get to weigh in since we're basically putting her in harm's way if we keep her home."

"I'm totally on board with staying put for now," Lily said. "You're right about this guy and how he's likely to react if I try to hide. I'm not willing to elevate my own personal safety if it means that he could act out by killing more women. I am capable of taking care of myself. And I'll have the help of Rex and the APD." Lily watched as Eliza's hazel eyes narrowed.

"Let me be clear, though," Derrick said. "We can't disregard your safety, Lily. Even if part of the plan is to try to catch or slow this guy down, we are going to be smart and cautious about it. We will add additional APD presence at your house, and of course Rex will still be with you. But at any point if we feel like the risk is too high, I'm reserving the right to pull you out of there. I appreciate your bravery, but we have to take a balanced approach in all of this."

"I understand that. But I'm not scared of this guy."

"Lily, how can you say that?" Eliza asked, clearly confused at Lily's response. "He's killed five women, not to mention he's come after you, too. I don't want you to take this threat lightly. This madman wants you dead. I simply can't stress enough the gravity of this situation. Just because you've been successful in evading him so far doesn't mean you're in the clear.

Far from it, actually." Eliza paused and then looked directly at her. "Is there a piece of this puzzle that I'm missing? If so, now would be the best time to fill me in. I can't work from partial information."

"Sean, can you give us a moment alone, please?" Derrick asked Sean.

"Sure, sir." Sean didn't question his boss and stood up to exit the room. Once the door was shut, Derrick looked at Lily.

"I think you should tell Eliza about your background," Derrick said. "This really isn't the time for her to operate without all the facts."

She considered it for a moment and realized that maybe revealing her history would be useful. It would also help to explain her reactions to the situation.

Lily looked over at Rex, and he nodded his agreement.

"I have the feeling, given the looks on all of your faces, that this is going to be important," Eliza said.

Well, here it goes, Lily thought. She'd see how Eliza took the news. "The short version is that I used to work for the CIA."

Eliza's eyes widened. "Well, that sure explains a lot." Eliza let out a breath. "Frankly, I'm glad to hear this because I was starting to wonder if there was something wrong with you. Now I see that isn't the case at all. I'm assuming you have specialized field training, as well?"

"Yes, I've been trained in advanced martial arts, self-defense, and I'm very capable with a gun and various other weapons."

"This complicates things. I'm assuming that someone has verified that there is no link between your past and the victims?" Eliza asked.

"We have," Rex said. "Zero connection to Lily's former life."

"This does add an interesting wrinkle to the equation. But, if anything, this helps us. If there are no links to the CIA, then that means our killer has no idea that he happened to pick a former CIA agent to mess with."

"That's right. And I want to use that to our advantage," Lily said. "The more he's preoccupied with finishing the job he started with me, the less time he can put into finding other women to kill. So if that means me lingering around to keep him interested, then I think that's the best course of action."

"I would tend to agree with you," Eliza said. "You're not an average woman, and we can use that to our advantage."

"I'll do whatever it takes to shut this guy down."

Sean walked back in the door, his face reddened. "I'm sorry to interrupt. But there's another dead body. He's struck again."

SIX

Lily felt sick to her stomach as she and Rex drove back home from the crime scene. Another innocent woman brutally murdered. A woman who bore an uncanny resemblance to her. This guy was proving that he didn't plan on stopping his killing spree anytime soon.

Rex let out a breath as he pulled into her driveway. Two police vehicles were there along with Alison's car.

"I need to tell my friends to stay away from me. I can't have this guy coming after them. He's proved that he's willing to kill with impunity. Even if his victims have all fit a certain profile, the fact that he shot you makes me think he'd do the same to my friends without a second's hesitation."

"I agree with you," Rex said. "But they're not going to like it."

She and Rex walked up to her front door and went inside. Alison had used her spare key and was waiting with Jackson in Lily's living room.

Her friends quickly stood and walked over to her. "We saw the news. Are you all right?"

"Yes, but unfortunately another woman is dead."

Alison pulled her in for a tight hug while Jackson eyed Rex warily. "You guys at the FBI need to be taking more action to catch this guy."

"They're doing everything they can, Jackson. He's proving to be very elusive."

"But they can do more," Alison pleaded. "They have to. You're not safe!"

"I know you two aren't going to like to hear this, but it's for your own good," Lily said.

"What?" Jackson asked.

"I need you two and Guy to steer clear of me for a while."

"But why?" Alison asked. "We can't just leave you to go through this alone."

"The killer is coming after anyone who is close to me. Rex is an obvious target, but this is his job."

"She's right," Rex said. "He's coming after Lily again. And while you aren't going to fit his profile, it won't matter. This killer doesn't have a conscience. If it means hurting you to get to Lily, then he wouldn't think twice about it."

"So until this is over, I'd prefer it if you wouldn't come over or try to see me. I'd never be able to live with myself if something happened to any of you."

Alison's dark eyes filled with tears. "This isn't fair, Lily."

"I know it's not, but I need you to be safe."

Alison gripped her hand. "I'm praying hard that this will end soon. That this murderer will be stopped."

"Thank you." Lily found no point in arguing with Alison over her prayers, but she feared that he was just getting started.

Later, Rex found Lily in the living room on the sofa while Grace slept by her feet, snoring up a storm.

"What's on your mind?" he asked. He could tell she was troubled, but who wouldn't be if they'd gone through what she had? It bothered him that he couldn't help her more. Because he really hated to see her so down.

"Just a bit upset about the latest victim. It's hard to deal with the fact that I'm still alive and well and the other victims are dead. All of them around my age, with their entire lives ahead of them. Why is my life continually being spared? How am I supposed to deal with that?"

"That's a heavy burden to carry, Lily, but it's not your fault. The killer is to blame. Not you. And the reason that you're still alive is because that's the plan God has for you."

"I'm not so sure about that, Rex." She paused. "And the killer has made it clear now that he has no intention of stopping." She put her head in her hands. "Coming after me is one thing. I know how to process that. But I'm having a much harder time processing the deaths of all those innocent women."

He moved closer to her on the couch. He felt the need to try to give her some measure of comfort, no matter how small. "Lily, you don't have to shoulder this all by yourself."

"I don't want you to think that I'm unappreciative. I know you're here and doing everything you can," she said softly.

"That's true, but that isn't what I meant." He knew that his abilities were limited.

"What, then?"

"You've made comments about faith before that make me think there's a story there. Maybe talking about it would make you feel at least a little bit better."

"But you know that my story doesn't have a happy ending." She looked up directly into his eyes.

He saw an emotion that wasn't just pain. No, it was raw anger. "I'm listening."

"It ends with me killing the man I thought I loved and who I thought loved me. What kind of God allows that to happen?" She asked in a raised voice. "Because I'd really like to hear your answer to that."

He took a moment to think about how best to address her concerns. "It doesn't really work like that, Lily."

"Then, how does it work?"

Before he could respond she kept on going.

"If you want to know what I'm feeling about faith, then I will tell you. I'm angry with God. Furious about the ordeal I went through with James. What I had to do. That I had to take a life after being horribly betrayed. And I've probably failed to mention in the midst of all of this that James actually professed to be a Christian."

"You surely can't paint all people of faith with one brush because of one bad man."

"I think he actually just lied about his religious beliefs to get closer to me. He knew that faith was something I cared about and so he played the part. Not a very hard thing to do for an elite-trained spy. It was as if he tore a page right out of the tradecraft playbook. And I fell for it all—hook, line and sinker."

"All of that is on James. It's not on God. The specific choices that James made and how he acted were a result of his individual free will. God didn't make him become a traitor. God didn't make him betray you. James did all of that on his own."

"That may be true, but frankly sometimes I wonder if God even exists. Things would make a lot more sense if He didn't. That would explain how messed up this world is."

He realized she wasn't holding back anymore. It was good to hear her getting out her emotions instead of leaving them bottled up.

"It's natural to be angry," he said.

"I'm more than angry. I'm livid. And I don't know how to really move on from what I've gone through. Especially if you expect me to be able to somehow reconcile with God."

"He's waiting for you, Lily. He hasn't gone anywhere."

"Assuming He was there to begin with."

He was going to take a chance and push her a little on this because he could see in her eyes where her heart lay. "Lily, I can tell you don't really mean what you say about God not existing."

She raised a curious eyebrow. "How in the world can you tell that?"

"Because we've been spending a great deal of time together, and, believe it or not, I've gotten to know a lot about you. You aren't making those statements with any level of conviction. You were just throwing it out there because you're hurting. Pain does that to people. Believe me, I know. I've been there."

"That doesn't change my anger, though, Rex. I'm still furious. And even though it's been nine months, the pain feels almost as raw as if it had happened yesterday." Her voice started to crack. "And now, on top of that, look at what has happened. If there is a God, then I'm really on His bad side, because I can't imagine He'd act like this to someone He really cared about."

Rex struggled to make sure he was going to say the right words. The last thing he wanted to do was shut down this conversation, but he felt Lily might have an incorrect perception of God's grace and love.

"Lily, God doesn't promise us that our lives following Him will be easy. If anything, we know that there will be many trials and tribulations along the way. The assurances made by Him aren't about our lives on earth."

"Yes, but that doesn't make it any easier to cope, does it?"

"What was your relationship with God like before everything happened with James?"

"I thought it was solid, but maybe I was wrong about that, too. I'm questioning everything these days."

"Were you going to church? Did you have a good support group of believers around you?"

She shook her head. "After college, I didn't go to church regularly. I traveled so much while I was in the CIA that it was hard to put down any roots. I was more of a 'do religion on my own' type of person. Kind of ironic that I was so successful as a CIA agent, because my natural inclination is to be introverted and keep only a very tight circle of friends around me."

"Maybe that's part of the problem, Lily. It's hard to go it alone. We need the help and support of others. Derrick has been a huge source of support and friendship for me. We both go to the same church. Judging by her comments, Alison is a believer. Can you lean on her?"

"Her faith is very strong. She grew up going to church, but I didn't. I didn't really get exposed to faith in any meaningful way until college. And I just never really talk about religion with anyone. The conversations I've had with you are more extensive than anything I've ever had."

"If you want to talk more, I'm here for whatever you need. But I don't want you to question God's love for you."

Grace barked loudly, providing a natural segue out of this conversation.

"We need to walk her," Lily said.

"Why don't you let me do it and you stay here."

"No, I'd like to get out, too."

"All right. I'll have another officer join us. Just to

be on the safe side." As he said the words, he wondered if there was such a thing as a safe side anymore.

Lily was awakened from a deep sleep by the sound of Grace barking loudly. Immediately, she knew something was terribly wrong.

She took in a deep breath and realized her bedroom was full of smoke.

Was she in a dream? As she fought to take another breath, she realized this was real. Her house was literally on fire. She didn't know how much time they had to escape the blaze—if any at all. Hopefully, it wouldn't be too late. How long had the flames been burning?

"Grace," she yelled. Her first priority was to try to grab Grace and get out of there. Right now! Every second that went by meant they were closer to being consumed by the deadly inferno.

And where was Rex? He would be downstairs sleeping in the guest room or keeping watch. There were no sounds of human voices in her room. Only loud, persistent barks from Grace and the crackling of wood that sounded like a fireplace on a cold winter's night.

As smoke continued to fill up her lungs, sending a burning sensation throughout her body, she crouched down on the ground and pulled Grace toward her. She crawled to the door and felt it. Hot. That meant the fire was coming from outside her room.

She was on the second floor of the house. Would jumping out of the window be possible? Maybe for her, but not for Grace. It was too far a drop. What was she going to do?

She found it harder and harder to breathe. But she had to get to the bedroom window and open it. Give them a fighting chance to survive this awful fire. A fire that had been no doubt set by the serial killer. There was no way this was random. Lily didn't believe in those types of coincidences.

Gathering every bit of strength she could, she pushed open the window and took in a deep breath of spring air. The fresh oxygen would also feed the flames if they reached her bedroom, but she had no choice. She and Grace had to take in some air or they would both pass out and be left for dead in the bedroom. Would help come? Would it be too late even if it arrived?

Grace kept barking, and in that moment she found herself doing something she told herself she wouldn't ever do again. *Lord, I know I just said I didn't need You. I also said I questioned Your existence. And if I die right now, I can deal with that. But please, God, save my dog, Grace. She's innocent in all of this. Don't punish her because of my flaws.*

Lily felt the temperature continue to rise in the room as tears fell down her face. She couldn't let Grace down. There had to be a way out.

That was when she heard Rex's voice coming from outside. A loud banging sound followed. A ladder.

She led Grace toward the window and saw Rex down below outside on a ladder.

"Lily, come on quickly," he yelled. "I'll get Grace after you get down."

"No way, Rex. Take her first. Then I'll come out."

He must have realized that she was serious because he didn't try to argue with her. Lily lifted Grace up and Rex grabbed her and handed her down to another man, who had just climbed up the ladder behind him.

Then Lily quickly stepped through the window and into Rex's arms before he placed her gently down on the rung of the ladder.

Not wasting any time, they both descended the ladder. Lily took each step focusing on holding on. Knowing that Grace was out of there safely made all the difference in the world.

Once her feet hit the ground, she was whisked away by Rex, but she looked over her shoulder and saw her house burning. A big Atlanta Fire Rescue Department truck had just arrived and firefighters were moving toward the house with large hoses. Huge plumes of smoke filled the air as the bright orange flames whipped back and forth in the wind.

She couldn't believe that this killer had tried to burn her house down. With her in it. Yes, her belongings could be replaced, although the home was her last tie to her family. But she and Grace were alive. Rex was alive. So for now all she could do was be thankful that no one had been killed. And that the Lord had answered her prayer.

Rex sat in the back of the ambulance, receiving oxygen for the smoke inhalation. He didn't even attempt to refuse the treatment because he knew for a fact that he needed it. This wasn't the time to play tough guy.

The firefighters now had the fire under control. It had all happened so fast. One minute he'd been asleep in the downstairs guest room, and the next he'd heard Grace barking. That was when he'd realized the house was on fire. He'd have to wait for the arson guys from the Atlanta Fire Rescue Department to tell him where the point of origin was. But wherever it was, it had been totally impossible for him to get up the steps. His path had been blocked by a huge wall of impenetrable flames. That moment of fear and total incapacity to help would be etched forever in his memory.

The only other way to get Lily and Grace to safety had been by going out the bedroom window. But for a moment there, it had been touch and go. So much for the killer having a cooling-off period.

What would the madman do when he found out Lily had survived? Certainly come after her again. He wouldn't give up his pursuit until he reached his ultimate objective.

He looked over at Lily. She was sitting in the back of the other ambulance with Grace right beside her. He noticed that she hadn't let go of Grace since they had gotten off that ladder.

She was talking to the paramedic about Grace's smoke inhalation. Rex knew it would be useless to tell her how she shouldn't have put Grace's well-being ahead of her own. That was just the type of person Lily was. Selfless. It was refreshing to be around someone like Lily. Rex had dealt with many people in his life who were just the opposite. It was all about them all the time. But not so with Lily.

Derrick walked over to him. "This was way too close a call."

"What is the fire department saying about the house?"

"I just spoke with one of the firefighters I know. He said there's a lot of damage. Because the call came in quick since there was security on the ground, it's not a total loss, but it will probably require a large renovation. I'm sure Lily has home insurance, but regardless, it's bad. There's no other way to sum it up."

"And it brings up the issue of where she's going to go now," Rex said.

"Even if the damage hadn't been this severe, I would've advocated moving her ASAP. I know that's ultimately your call since you're running point, but this guy has moved past the game phase to the actually-trying-to-kill-her phase." Derrick shook his head. "This guy is deadly. Calculating and brutal."

"Although you could say that if he was really paying attention, which I'm sure he is, then he would've thought that there was at least a decent chance that Lily would survive. He knows we have security in and around her house. Maybe this was a power play. Get her out of her home. Show her who's boss. Maybe he's annoyed that she hasn't shown any fear, and this was his attempt at trying to terrify her."

"Good observation, Rex."

He looked up and saw Eliza standing in front of him. "I just heard the last thing you said."

"Good, I'm glad you're here," Rex said. "What are your thoughts on what happened?"

"The first and most obvious question is how did it happen?" Eliza threw her hands up in the air. "How did this guy get past the security detail? Isn't that why the team is here, to protect Lily? This is unacceptable."

He'd never seen Eliza so animated.

"We're trying to run that down," Derrick said. "But at first glance, it appears it was a combination of technological manipulation and his ability to detain a couple of our guys through some type of diversion."

Eliza stood, all five feet of her, tapping her foot.

"What're you thinking?" Rex asked.

"Is there any way that our guy could have a connection to law enforcement?"

"Whoa," Derrick said. He put his hand up. "You can't step in here and start accusing my guys of murder just because there was a security breakdown tonight. There's a big difference between a mistake and cold-blooded murder. None of them is capable of this type of thing. Believe me, I know these guys. They would never kill innocent women."

"Just calm down, Derrick," she responded. "I realize that you are loyal to your officers, but you need to be more impartial about this."

"She's right," Rex said. "We have six innocent victims. Who knows when he's going to kill again? Plus, we can't forget he set fire to Lily's house while he knew good and well she was in there. We have to consider every possible scenario here. Even if it's one that makes you and me very uncomfortable."

"And you left the part out where he tried to kill you, too," Eliza said to Rex.

Derrick took a step closer to him. "If we're going to look at law enforcement, then we need to look at FBI, too."

Eliza nodded. "I wasn't insinuating otherwise. All of our people need to be checked out. But this conversation doesn't go any further than the three of us. No one on our teams needs to hear about this yet. Because if I'm right, the likelihood that the person is here right now is high. We need to do an initial assessment first."

Rex nodded. "Agreed."

"All right. I can deal with that," Derrick said. "Although I'm not jumping to any conclusions about my officers. I need to see solid evidence."

"Understood," Eliza said. "None of us wants this to be the case. It's just a possibility that I can't turn a blind eye to."

"Back to what we do from here and your thoughts on what this guy's overall plan is," Derrick said.

"I think this was an act to terrorize Lily," she said. "Our killer is on point. He's methodical in his approach. He had to have known that it would be likely she'd get out alive, given the police presence."

"So he's trying to make a point?" Derrick asked.

"He wants to strip Lily of everything and everyone she cares about. This was a direct personal hit. What's more personal than your home? Nothing."

"And he succeeded. The house is severely damaged," Rex said. "He's trying to show her that she may have gotten away from him the first time, but now he has the power to wreak havoc on her life."

"I have to bring this up, as I'm looking over at Lily now," Eliza said. "It's evident me that her dog is special to her. Our killer knows that, too. I wouldn't put it past him to go after the dog."

"It seems to me that it's time to take Lily to an FBI safe house," Derrick said. "I know she won't leave Grace behind, so the dog will come, as well."

"How do you think she'll take the news?" Eliza asked.

"Well, given the circumstances with her house, she probably will realize that there isn't much of an alterative," Rex said. "And, like you said, Derrick, as long as she isn't separated from Grace, I think she will be fine."

"I can start working on that from our side at the Bureau," Eliza said. "What else can I do?"

"Figure out a way to crack this case," Rex said. "Before anyone else dies."

Lily had insisted on checking into a dog-friendly hotel while the FBI sorted out the best safe house for her and Grace to be moved to. There was no way she was going to part from her dog, especially given all that Grace had been subjected to.

The night before, Eliza had shared her opinion

with Lily about what the killer was trying to accomplish with the fire. After thinking about it until the early-morning hours, she tended to agree. Everything this guy was doing was to get at her. Physically and mentally. Eliza had also shared with Lily her concern that the killer would come after Grace.

That thought made Lily sick. Lily promised to herself that she would fight to the death to protect that animal. Because Grace was so much more than just a dog to her. Grace was her loyal companion.

Lily had closed her eyes a few times, but basically no more sleep had come. Now the sun shone brightly through the hotel window. Rex was next door in the adjoining room. And Grace had just been walked by two police officers, who had assured Lily that they would keep Grace safe. They wouldn't allow Lily out of the hotel, as they said the FBI had deemed it too dangerous.

She jumped at the sound of the knock at the door joining her room with Rex's. This killer had her on edge, and it wasn't a place she was accustomed to being.

Taking a deep breath, she walked over and opened the door, letting Rex in. Grace welcomed him with tail wags and a hearty bark.

"How you doing, girl?" he asked Grace.

He knelt down and gave her some rubs as Grace licked his face. Lily couldn't help but smile. If she had to be in this position, at least it was with someone who shared her love for dogs.

"And how are you doing?" Rex asked her. His

brown eyes showed his concern, but the dark circles under his eyes also let her know that they'd had a very similar night.

"I'm okay. Have you heard anything yet about the safe house?"

"Yes. We should be moving there within the hour."

"With Grace, right?" Even though it was more of a statement than a question, because she'd told anyone who would listen that there was no way she was leaving Grace behind.

"Of course. I heard you loud and clear on that request. We're going to keep both of you safe and secure. I wouldn't try to separate you from Grace unless your life depended on it."

Instead of arguing the point with him, she decided to move on to another very important topic. "Have you checked on my friends to make sure that they are okay, too?"

"Yes. They each got a personal visit from the Atlanta police this morning. They've been apprised of the situation with your house and the fire."

"You're sure that they're all right?"

"Yes. But you should know that they will not know your location, which is to protect everyone involved."

"As long as they're safe." She paused. "Do you think we could get them police protection?"

He shook his head. "Until there's something actionable going on as far as they are concerned, we won't be able to assign any specific security detail to them. We're always battling a resource issue."

"Put the former CIA operative in a safe house

while leaving the untrained civilians to fend for themselves. Great." She couldn't help the sarcasm that she knew she was projecting.

"I get that you're upset, Lily. But this is the best we can do under this set of circumstances." He reached out and grabbed her hand.

She flinched. Not because she was afraid of him, but just because she wasn't used to the contact. But his touch actually provided comfort. "I don't want to sound unappreciative. Especially to you. You've put your entire life on hold for this case."

"It's what I do. So don't feel bad about it."

"When I realized that the house was on fire and I was stuck in the bedroom with Grace, I came to the conclusion that it could be the end of the line for me."

"And how did you feel in that moment?" He squeezed her hand before letting go.

"Honestly, a combination of emotions. But mostly I could accept the fact that I was going to die. I've been in very dangerous situations before. Not just what happened with James when I knew for certain that if I didn't take the shot he was going to kill me, but other CIA missions that were just as dangerous." She took a breath and fought back her emotions. "But when I looked at Grace and thought about how innocent she was and how she was only in that situation because of me, I did something I haven't done since before I had to kill James in self-defense."

"What did you do?"

She took a deep breath, feeling some of the tension melt away. "In that moment, I actually prayed."

His dark eyes softened. "Isn't that a good thing?"

"I don't know how I feel about it now. At the time, I felt as if I might not be worth saving. That God was done with me. But I thought that He might have mercy on an innocent animal. So I prayed for Grace's life to be spared." She exhaled loudly. "And so I'm thankful that we both made it out alive. I'm almost in shock that He answered my prayer."

"God hasn't abandoned you, Lily. I can tell that you think He has, but He hasn't."

She nodded. "I appreciate you saying that. Even if I have a hard time processing all my feelings about faith right now."

"Just take it one day at a time."

"I feel as if you've seen me so exposed and know my struggles. I barely know anything about you."

He grinned. "I've been told that I'm a very private person."

She laughed. "I am, too, but given what's happened I haven't exactly had that option."

"What would you like to know about me?"

"You obviously love Grace. Why don't you have a dog of your own?"

"My schedule. I work such crazy, long hours. I didn't think it would be fair to be an absentee pet parent. Especially when it's just me, and the dog would be totally dependent."

"You said you choose to be alone, though."

"Yes. It works for me."

"Why do I sense that you have a story, too? Probably nothing as dramatic as mine with James, but there's something that happened to you, isn't there?"

He took a seat on one of the two hotel room chairs. "Sit down."

She sat down and looked at him, awaiting what he had to say.

"I don't talk about this with anyone, but you're right. You've had to expose so much to me. I think it's only fair I return the favor. Especially since we're going to be stuck together for a while."

"I'm all ears."

"I proposed to my high school sweetheart after we graduated. The plan was that we'd go to college and get married at some point during school or right after. In my mind, it was exactly how I'd envisioned it going."

"I have the feeling that this isn't going to have a happy ending, is it?"

He shook his head. "No. She accepted my proposal but then a week later she broke it off."

"Why?"

"She'd been cheating on me with my best friend."

"Oh, no, Rex. I'm so sorry. The betrayal must have been so intense."

He ran a hand through his hair. "It was. At least she eventually had the decency to come clean. It would've been nice if it would've been before I got down on one knee and professed my love to her. But still."

"And your friend?"

"We literally haven't spoken since. And that was ten years ago. He found out that she talked to me, and then he didn't even have the decency to face me man-to-man. Shaken up by the betrayal, I actually changed my college plans and went to Athens. I needed to get out of this town and away from them."

"That's awful. He surely wasn't much of a friend. Friends don't do that to each other."

"Looking back, my girlfriend and I were probably too young to get married. But it didn't change the hurt I felt at the time. It was so raw. Then I shifted my focus to school and my career. I figured if the Lord ever wanted me to be with someone, He'd make it obvious to me."

"And I take it, then, it hasn't been obvious to you?"

"Not at all. There's been no one truly special since then. But believe it or not, I'm okay with that. His plan is greater than any plan of mine. I put my trust in Him and walk where He leads me."

"You have a lot more faith than I'll ever have. I have to say it's an admirable quality."

"With the heinous stuff I see in my line of work, it's a necessity."

"Thanks for sharing," she said. "Now I don't feel as if things are so one-sided. But you've still seen a lot more of my baggage than I've seen of yours."

His phone rang and he pulled it out. After a minute he hung up. "We've been given the green light for the safe house. It's go time."

SEVEN

Rex pasted on a confident smile, although inside he felt anything but. He looked down at his hands gripping the wheel of the car and hoped that Lily hadn't picked up on his apprehension. He couldn't help being worried about the situation and Lily's personal security. If something happened to her, it would be on his watch. And he couldn't let that happen.

He glanced in the rearview mirror and saw that their security escort was right behind him in a dark SUV, just as they were supposed to be. Another vehicle was two cars ahead of them. Everything was going according to plan.

They were currently en route to the FBI safe house that had been assigned to them. Lily seemed to be holding up pretty well, considering that she could have been killed in last night's house fire.

"You're awfully quiet," Lily said. "What are you thinking?"

"Always trying to put the pieces of the puzzle together. And while we have some time completely alone here in the car, there's something I wanted to share with you."

"Uh-oh. Why all the secrecy?"

He felt she didn't deserve to be in the dark. "Once I tell you, you'll understand why." He took a breath. "Because Eliza thinks that our killer could be connected to law enforcement."

"What?" she asked loudly, which then led to Grace barking from the backseat. "It's okay, Grace. Settle down." She paused. "Anyway, is Eliza implying someone in the FBI is responsible for this?"

"Well, she's not limiting it to the FBI. She's considering FBI, Atlanta Police, anyone currently working or connected to your case that's in law enforcement."

Lily blew out a breath. "An inside job."

"Basically. But at this point it's just a working theory. There is currently no evidence linking any member of the investigative team to these crimes."

"And what do you think about it?"

He glanced over at her and then turned his focus back to the road. He couldn't afford to be distracted. "I think we have to consider it. The guy definitely has skills. The fact that he's been able to avoid detection this long, and breach our defenses and safeguards, makes me wonder if there is something to it. It makes me sick to think about the possibility, but I have to be objective here. I can't allow my feelings about law enforcement to cloud my judgment. It's entirely possible there's one bad apple in the bunch."

"Well, it might explain some things. Just like last night with the fire. If it was someone on the inside, they could've gotten through the security measures much easier. Access wouldn't have been an issue."

"That's true." As he listened to her words, he admitted that his mind had gone through the same ideas.

"Or what if they were just posing as law enforcement?" she asked. "With both FBI and APD on the case, I wouldn't rule that out, because there would be a lot of unfamiliar faces working together."

"That's an interesting point. Eliza is going to run a separate internal investigation. The only people that know about it are her, Derrick and me—and now you. We've kept the circle incredibly tight because we can't afford any possible exposure to the culprit. Assuming this theory has any legs."

"I won't say anything," she said.

"I know you wouldn't." He smiled. "I think a CIA agent knows how to keep secrets."

"How much security do we have with us now on the way to the safe house?" She turned and looked out the back window.

"Two cars are escorting us on our way there. But we've taken a circular route to ensure that no one is following us. And, as an extra layer of precaution, we sent out decoy cars in other directions. The whole point of the safe house is to keep your location classified. If the killer finds out where you are, then hiding out is completely pointless."

"You know I can't run forever, though. And what am I going to do about my house?"

"Right now it's an active arson scene. Once the investigation is complete, I'm sure your insurance adjustor will contact you with the next steps."

"My photography is really going to have to take off if I'm going to be able to afford a full renovation of that house." She laughed. "It's not funny, but it's better to laugh than to cry. At least we're alive. So I can't really complain, given the circumstances."

"That's the most important thing to remember. Stuff can be replaced."

"Believe me, I am thankful."

He wound his way through a middle-class neighborhood in the Atlanta suburbs and then stopped when he got to the address. The two-story brick home in a cozy neighborhood was perfect for their purpose.

"It's been a while since I've been to a safe house. The ones I remember from the CIA weren't always this nice." She looked over at him and smiled.

"I can imagine that you weren't in the middle of an American suburb, either."

"You'd be right about that."

"But you can't reveal more details about your locations or operations."

"You catch on quick. Everything was need-to-know and top secret."

"That's a stressful way to live, Lily."

"Yeah, it was. But at the time I enjoyed it." She paused. "Well, until, you know, I got betrayed and everything that went along with it."

"I think anyone would feel that way."

"What happens now?" she asked.

"We're going to wait in the car while the security detail makes sure the house is secure."

"All right."

"Do you miss it?" he asked.

"Miss what?"

"The CIA."

"Ah. I guess you could say it depends. You know there are definite parts about it that I miss. But the continuous subterfuge got old. Photography is so soothing to me. It puts me in a good place mentally and emotionally. Capturing beauty in so many different ways, through so many different lenses, fulfills me, gives me a sense of peace."

"Being an agent in the field must take a huge emotional toll even without the extreme circumstances you dealt with."

"Yeah, burnout is a big problem for operatives. Along with a variety of substance-abuse problems. Thankfully, I never dealt with that. I was pretty good at compartmentalization. Especially after I saw how drugs and alcohol impacted my mother. That was just one road I wasn't ever going to go down, if I could help it. I think in the end getting out was the best decision."

"Did they want you to stay after what happened?"

"Actually, yes. My boss gave me a huge guilt trip."

"I want to say that I can't believe it, but the CIA has quite the reputation for being a very difficult place to work. I know the FBI has its faults, too, but the Agency is a different animal."

"Yeah, the conversation with him will be something I always replay in my mind. He told me that I would've killed James in vain if I didn't keep fighting the good fight."

"That's an awful thing to say to you. Especially after what you'd just gone through."

"It was. But that was the Agency mentality. My boss didn't get to where he was by having a soft heart. He had to always think of the mission before the individual people. In his mind, I was a hero for killing off a traitor. He didn't have to live through actually shooting someone he loved. I'm the one who had to bear that burden."

"Do you want to talk about it?" He watched as two FBI agents walked toward the house while an APD officer stood watch.

"I reacted the only way I could under the circumstances. The look in James's green eyes when he realized that I knew he was a double agent is something I'll hold with me forever. For what it's worth, he said he was sorry. That he didn't want it to end like that. Then he went for his gun. But I was faster. I don't think he ever even considered that I would take the first shot. He assumed I loved him too much to save myself, that I'd never pull the trigger."

"You acted in self-defense. That was the only thing you could do to survive."

"I know that. But I had so many unanswered questions, you know? Like, was our entire relationship a ruse? Did he just use me to further his own agenda? Did he care for me at all? And then, on top of all of that, how could I have not known? It made me very angry. At everything."

Before he could stop himself, he reached out to grab her hand. "Lily, you don't have to hold all of it in. I'm here if you want to talk it out or just vent. I think we're very similar in the way we handle our emotions. I know what it's like to bottle everything up, and I also know that it's very unhealthy to live like that."

"Thank you, Rex. I'm sure that I haven't fully processed what happened in a healthy way. I've just done the best I could."

He could hear the sound of determination in her voice. This woman was a fighter. She wasn't going to give up. He watched as the FBI agent came out of the house and gave the all clear.

"Looks as if we're good to go," she said.

"Yeah. Let's get inside and then we can have Grace walked."

"Thanks for listening, Rex."

He looked into her bright blue eyes and seriously started to wonder if he was beginning to have feelings for this woman.

Lily hadn't been outside in two days. It was driving her nuts being cooped up in the house. Granted, it was a lovely home, but she couldn't help feeling claustrophobic. They wouldn't even let her walk her own dog. But at least Grace was there with her and being cared for, getting multiple long walks each day with the officers.

The safe house itself had been a hub of activity

with FBI agents and APD officers coming and going. She'd gotten word that somehow her most expensive camera had survived the fire. And while the damage to her house wasn't quite as severe as she had expected, the renovations were still going to cost a fortune because insurance only covered so much.

But she really couldn't worry about those details right now. She had bigger problems. She looked over at Rex, who sat across from her at the kitchen table. Her stomach rumbled, and she started to think about dinner.

They were both working on their laptops. He was presumably doing work, and she was messing around with editing some digital photos. Her heart really wasn't in it. It was just something to pass the time. How could she really be focused on her work when the killer was still out there and probably ready to strike again?

The FBI had provided her with their encryption program that was used at safe houses so that she could log into her email and not have to worry about the killer tracking her location.

But as she refreshed her email box, her stomach dropped.

"Rex, I think you should see this." Her eyes scanned the message quickly and she let out a breath.

He stood up and walked around to her side of the table. Leaning down toward her, he read it out loud—"'You can't hide forever. If you try to stay hidden, the killing will continue and it will all be your fault.'"

"So now he's threatening to kill more women if I don't come out of hiding," she said.

Rex blew out a breath. "Lily, he's going to keep killing women regardless. You and I both know that. This contact is all just part of his mind game. He's trying to break you down, scare you. Make you act irrationally."

She looked up into his dark eyes. "I think we should talk to Eliza again about me making contact with him."

"We can talk to her, but I don't think she's going to be on board. And I can't say I think it's the greatest idea, either. We can't presume that this guy is a rational actor. That he would act like a normal functioning human being under a different set of circumstances."

He went back around and took a seat at his computer. "Forward me the message and I'll send it on for analysis. I'm sure he's covered his electronic tracks, but that won't stop us from looking."

"Sending now." She took a moment to gather her thoughts. "Hear me out about this."

"I'll listen to what you have to say. You can always tell me what you're thinking."

"If I could make contact with him, maybe that would stave him off for a bit. He'll be so interested in continuing the conversations with me and less interested on killing."

"Or, the alternative is that talking to you will amp this guy up so much that he has to go out there and immediately find another victim."

"Like Eliza said at the meeting, it's a calculated

risk. You yourself just said that he's going to keep killing. The only thing that will stop him is us catching him. But in the meantime, what if my emailing or texting him could keep him occupied for a little bit? Even if it only takes him away from killing for one day you never know how that would impact things. Don't you think we should try to buy time in any way we can?"

"Eliza is actually already on her way over and should be here any minute. We'll talk about this with her, in addition to our normal updates. I'm sure she'll have an opinion."

Lily reached down and patted Grace while she thought about the email that the killer had sent her. "It's strange, though," she said, thinking out loud.

"What?"

"The killer had to know if he attempted to burn down my house that I would have to leave if any level of damage was sustained. Did he miscalculate? Did he fail to factor in the possibility of me being moved to a safe house?"

Rex walked to the refrigerator and pulled out a can of soda. "Would you like one?"

"Sure," she said.

He handed her the soda can and took his seat. "You raise a good point. But maybe he thought he was so on top of things that he'd be able to track you once you left your house. Maybe he was watching and waiting, but then he got thrown off the trail because of all the chaos. Or he could've been worried about being caught. One thing I can say about this guy is that he is arrogant. He has an ego, thinks he can out-smart us. He prides himself on being one step ahead of law enforcement. Believes that he knows the system better than we do."

"And he may very well be in law enforcement," Eliza said as she strode into the kitchen. Her long, dark hair flowed down past her shoulders today instead of being pulled back, and she was wearing glasses for the first time that Lily had seen.

"Eliza, before we go down that road, I need to tell you that I got an email from the killer."

"I just saw that on my BlackBerry as I was walking in. He's really desperate for contact. First the text messages, now email. Even if it's only a virtual connection, he still knows that he's getting his message through to you."

"Don't you think we should consider the possibility of me responding to him?"

Eliza smoothed down her navy suit jacket and took a seat at the table alongside Rex. "We can talk about it, but I'd like to discuss some updates on my other investigation. We're the only ones in this part of the house so we can speak freely. I think you'll find the developments of great interest."

"What did you find out?" Rex asked.

"We're still examining the initial evidence. So I don't want to name names just yet, but I can tell you that there is a possible lead. It would actually make sense in many ways if it pans out."

"But you can't tell us who it is?" Lily asked. That was annoying. She hated being left in the dark. Especially when it literally impacted her life. "Don't you think I deserve to know who it is, Eliza?"

"Soon. Believe me, I get that you're anxious and you have every right to be. I just need to verify a few more things. But if this lead does hold up, we could be making an arrest within days. I don't think I have to tell you how huge that would be for you, Lily."

"And what if it doesn't pan out?" Rex asked. "We need a contingency plan."

Lily jumped in. "Which is why I want you to let me respond to this email. I think it could be helpful, and I hate feeling so helpless. I'd make sure the wording was carefully vetted through you and anyone else you deemed appropriate."

Eliza held up her hand. "Everyone just needs to take a deep breath. Or better yet, a series of deep breaths. I can tell that you want to take action, Lily, and I sympathize with your position. It's hard being locked up in here day in and day out, especially given your background, but we have to think about the bigger picture. And if you just give me a little time to do my job, then we'll get through this. I'm not asking for much here and the stakes are high. I'm so close, let's not mess up the approach by getting impatient when it counts the most."

Lily didn't want to wait. She had to be reasonable, though. Eliza's reaction made Lily think that not only was Eliza close to taking action against a suspect, but that she was very confident that this was the guy. That she'd found the killer. Lily would withhold judgment until she had all the facts and evidence in front of her.

Eliza stood and buttoned up her suit jacket. "I hate to run so quickly, but I need to try to finish up analyzing the evidence we have. The sooner I can make a call on that, the sooner we can all move forward with the investigation, no matter the outcome. Our tech team is on the email tracing, but we suspect the perp used a complex IP masking system just as he did with the other communications. So I wouldn't hold your breath on that."

"Let me know as soon as you have something concrete," Rex said.

"Will do." Eliza bent down to give Grace a few rubs. "Hang tight, Lily. Hopefully this will be over soon."

Eliza walked out of the kitchen and Lily looked over at Rex. "So what did you think about all of that?"

He ran a hand through his hair and leaned back in the kitchen chair. "I think she believes she has this guy nailed, but just wants to cover all of her bases before an arrest is made."

"Why do I sense some skepticism from you?"

"I'm just trying to be cautious. And of course, I'd rather not have a situation where one of my people at the FBI or someone at APD is a serial killer."

"Guess we'll just have to wait until Eliza share's the evidence she's been gathering." Her thoughts were interrupted by commotion at the front door.

"Sounds as if dinner's here. And not a moment too soon—I'm starving," Rex said.

Just then, one of the APD officers came into the kitchen carrying a tall stack of pizza boxes. Lily had been craving pineapple and extra cheese, which was her absolute favorite, so she got her own special order. Everyone else in the house wanted the works or extra meat.

"Thank you so much," she said. She took a small box from the top of the stack, and the officer placed the other larger boxes on the kitchen counter.

"You're welcome, ma'am. Sean picked up the order and just dropped it off. He wanted me to tell you that he checked on your friends again on the way over here and that everyone was doing just fine. He knew that you'd be worried about their well-being."

Her heart was filled with relief as she pulled out paper plates and napkins from the kitchen cabinet for herself and Rex. "That's great news. I needed to hear something positive."

"Let me know if you two need anything else," the officer said.

She watched as Grace eyed the pizza boxes on the counter. "Don't even think about it, Grace."

"You've got to keep your eye on her." Rex laughed. "But she's fully stocked with her own dog food and it's the brand you requested. One of the agents made a pet-store run."

They'd been feeding her a generic food that Lily wasn't too fond of. Now she was glad that Grace would be back to her regular diet. One that didn't include pizza. "I'm trying to do my best not to totally spoil her with things like people food."

"She's a good dog. I can see her catching on already to the training. And she's been through so much since you were attacked the first night. You should be proud of her. She's a real trouper."

As if Grace could tell they were talking about her, she stood tall and started wagging her tail. "That's a good girl, Grace. But you're still not eating my pizza. Or Rex's pizza."

Rex took out two enormous slices of extra-meat pizza and put them on his plate. She opened her small box and pulled out her pineapple and extra cheese. It smelled wonderful—the perfect mix of cheese, marinara and pineapple with a hint of garlic.

Not wasting any time, she took a huge bite. The tangy marinara sauce hit her tongue. It had a bit of a kick to it, but she was so hungry she didn't mind. She took another bite and looked up at Rex. He had already polished off his first piece and was moving on to the second.

"Does yours taste a little strange?" she asked.

He shook his head. "Tastes like regular pizza to me."

She took another small bite, and then put the rest of the piece down. "Mine has a weird flavor."

He set down his piece. "What do you mean?"

"It just tastes strange. At first I thought it was just me, but I don't think so anymore."

His eyes widened and he jumped up from his seat and yanked the pizza from the table.

"What are you doing?"

"Your pizza. We can't risk it."

"Risk what?" And as the words came out of her

mouth, a wave of intense nausea swept over her. "I think I'm going to be sick."

Rex pulled out his phone, and she could hear him requesting medical help ASAP.

Her brain became foggy. She tried to focus on her breathing, but she felt as if she were drowning. Maybe if she closed her eyes it would all be okay. Darkness made everything easier.

Rex rushed over to Lily's unconscious body, which was slumped over in her chair. *Dear Lord, please let her be okay.*

"We need help now!" he yelled.

Another FBI agent rushed into the room. "Paramedics are less than five minutes out."

"I don't know if she has five minutes to spare." His mind raced as he thought about the possibility of Lily dying right there in front of him in the FBI safe house. He had to push those negative feelings out of his mind.

Another agent and an Atlanta police officer rushed in, but Rex was on autopilot trying to take care of Lily until professional medical help arrived. They'd all received basic medical training because of their jobs, but he feared she was going to need experts.

He carefully lifted Lily out of the chair and laid her down gently on the kitchen floor. "Get me some cool towels," he said to the other agent. He watched helplessly as the color drained out of Lily's face. They were truly in a race against the clock. If she'd ingested some type of poison, a doctor would have to determine if it was better to induce vomiting or not. He had no idea what the right thing to do was. All he could do was pray. He let out a breath when the paramedic arrived and started to work on Lily.

"Rex, what in the world happened here?" Derrick strode into the room and looked down at Lily. Then he knelt down beside her.

"I think she was poisoned," Rex said. As the words came out of his mouth, he still couldn't believe it. Never in his wildest imagination had he thought that they needed to screen her food.

"But how?" Derrick asked with wide blue eyes.

"That's the million-dollar question. The killer had to have had access to the food. It was her pizza. She complained that it tasted strange. But how did the killer know who to follow to be able to get access to her food?"

"This all points to an inside job," Derrick said. "I didn't want to think that was possible, but how could it be anything else?"

The EMT continued to work on Lily as Rex and Derrick looked on.

"Her blood pressure is dropping," the EMT said. "We have to get her transferred to the ER immediately. I've started a line for IV fluid, but we need testing to determine what we're dealing with here. The doctors could take a variety of approaches if they think she's ingested something poisonous."

"Derrick and I will ride along in the ambulance with you," Rex told the paramedic. "There's no way we're leaving her alone with you. It's too dangerous for her, and for you and the driver."

"Understood," the man said. "Let's move."

Once inside the ambulance, Rex watched as the EMT continued to check her vitals.

"We've got to be more careful," Derrick said. "And we've got to figure out where the breakdown in our security occurred."

"I just pray that she makes it through the night," Rex said.

"Me, too," Derrick responded. "The Lord was already watching over her, though. She stopped eating. If she'd had more of the pizza, who knows what would've happened?"

"We were supposed to protect her, man. We let her down."

Derrick hung his head. "Believe me, I know. We'll get through this and make sure nothing else happens to her."

"I'm going to hold you to that," Rex said. "And I'm holding myself accountable, as well."

"We never could've known the psychopathic killer would've taken this route."

"With this guy I think we've learned one very deadly fact. Absolutely nothing is off the table."

EIGHT

The next morning, Rex watched as Lily lay still in the hospital bed. It had been a long night. That had been one close call. Just as Derrick had surmised, the doctor had told him that if she'd eaten the entire piece of pizza that she'd most likely be dead by now.

They were still determining the exact type of poison used, but at the end of the day it didn't really matter. What mattered was that Lily had almost been killed—in the safe house and literally sitting right in front of him. He kicked himself for not being more careful regarding the food. Honestly, poisoning hadn't even been on his radar.

What bothered him even more was how the killer had gained access to her food in the first place. There were too many unanswered questions. Lily's eyes opened and locked on his.

He walked over and grabbed on to her hand. "You're going to be okay, Lily."

"What happened?" she asked in a raspy voice.

"You were right about your pizza tasting strange. You were poisoned."

She sucked in a breath. "Yes, I'm remembering now. I'm so thankful that I didn't eat more than I did."

"Me, too. You had me worried there for a second when you blacked out. They're giving you fluids because you did get sick once they transferred you here. But that's actually good because it was better than keeping the poison in your system."

She nodded. "What are we going to do now?"

"There's a lot of stuff happening behind the scenes. Eliza said she didn't want to reveal anything over the phone, but that she'd be coming by here to check on you and to talk to us about next steps."

"Is Grace all right?"

"Yes, she's at the safe house, under the care of an agent I know personally."

"Was my pizza the only one that was poisoned?"

"Yes. This attack was specifically targeted at you. The killer knew which pizza was yours."

"And how did the killer track me down?"

"Believe me, I have the same questions. We have people looking into all of this right now, trying to figure out which methods he used to find you."

Eliza rushed through the door looking as if she hadn't slept. Her hair was falling out of its bun and her glasses did nothing to cover up the dark circles under eyes. "I have news," Eliza said. "But first, Lily, thank God you're okay." The agent walked over and gave her hand a strong squeeze.

"What is the news?" Rex asked, cutting right to it.

"I just spoke with the prosecutor on the case, Steffie Hood. She's about to press charges against Officer Sean Bishop. He's being brought in as we speak."

"What?" Lily and Rex said in unison.

"You think that Sean Bishop is the killer?" Rex asked. "That seems highly unlikely."

"I thought so at first, too, but there's mounting evidence against him. It's definitely enough for him to be charged at this point."

"What evidence?" Rex asked. "First of all, how did Sean attack Lily and then drive me to the scene minutes later?" They were way off base here. This just wasn't right.

"We're thinking that there's an accomplice," Eliza said. "That Sean was working with someone else. What we don't know yet is whether that person is also inside the APD. The investigation is ongoing, and we're hoping that Sean will give up his accomplice through the interrogation process."

"So what exactly do you have on Sean?" Rex asked. "Beyond conjecture. I'm talking about real, hard evidence." It already sounded as if there were holes in Eliza's theory from the first step, and Rex didn't like holes.

"An electronic trail for one. Our people at the FBI were finally able to discover some cracks in the system and trace the communications back to Sean."

"Can't those be faked?" Lily asked. "Especially if the person has strong computer skills."

"Yes, but it's not just the texts and email. His DNA was found at one of the murder scenes. And he didn't work that scene. So there's no other possible explanation for why his DNA would be there."

Rex shook his head, desperately trying to process this impossible development. Could it be conceivable that Sean was a serial killer who had been targeting Lily? Rex hadn't known Sean that long, but he definitely didn't fit his profile of what this killer would be like.

"Are you sure?" Lily asked.

"There are too many pieces of evidence against him. Not to mention that he was the one who picked up your pizza last night. Which means he had the opportunity to poison it after he left the restaurant. It all adds up once you look at everything and connect the dots."

Lily sucked in a breath. "This is too much. It just makes no sense. Why would Sean put himself in that type of position to pick up the pizza if he was the killer and trying to poison me?"

Eliza took a few steps closer and touched Lily's arm. "Lily, even the most skilled killers become emotional and make bad decisions. And you've been through a tremendous amount of trauma, and I understand that this must be very disconcerting for you. Someone you trusted with your security may very well be the actual threat. But this is a huge step. The only missing piece is the identity of Sean's accomplice. Once that is revealed, you'll be completely safe. And we have every reason to believe that Sean is the biggest threat. In my opinion, it's likely that he may have hired someone to attack you in your home. We are executing a search warrant at Sean's house right now. So hopefully we'll know more soon. But this is exactly the break we needed."

Rex wasn't just going to roll with Eliza's theories. He had to protect Lily until he was certain that they had the right guy. "Eliza, you should understand one thing. Until I am satisfied that the threat is over, I'm not leaving Lily. All the evidence you speak of could still be manipulated. Even DNA. You know that as well as I do."

Eliza leaned up against the hospital wall, propping up one foot to balance herself. "I appreciate that you are being cautious. But I wanted to share my findings with you as soon as I could. I spoke to Derrick on the way over here. He's understandably distressed, given that Sean is one of his direct reports. For the time being, we're only going to use FBI for the majority of the security detail. Once everyone in the APD involved with the case has been thoroughly vetted, they will be rotated back in."

"I'm all for being thorough," Rex said. He just hoped they weren't looking for answers in the wrong place.

Eliza's phone rang, and she looked down. "It's the prosecutor. I need to take this. I'll check back in with you later."

Eliza walked out, leaving him alone with Lily.

"When did the doctor say I could be discharged?" she asked.

"Later today. Once you get all the fluids he ordered."

"I don't like hospitals, and I've been in them twice lately. Two times too many."

He looked at her. She'd been through a lot. The poison and her resulting illness had left her skin pale. But there was still a spark in her blue eyes. A strength that drew him toward her. A feeling he was totally unable to explain. "Try to get some rest. You can't speed up the fluid intake. I'll be right here."

"Thank you for not leaving me," Lily said. "I don't care if they think they caught the guy. It's going to take a lot more than what Eliza said for me to feel safe."

As Lily sat in the living room of the new safe house that night, she fought back tears. She'd always considered herself a very strong, independent person. She'd been tested in the field as a CIA agent numerous times. But she'd never experienced anything like this before, and admittedly it was beginning to take its toll on her. She was physically and emotionally spent.

She honestly didn't know what else to do but pray. Granted, God might not want to hear from her, but she was close to rock bottom. And there was something telling her that it was time to really try to reach back out to God. Her faith path had been winding, with many hills and valleys, but all she could understand at this point in time was that she couldn't keep going it alone. The big question was, how would God receive her prayers?

Taking a deep breath, she prayed. *Lord, please help me get through this ordeal, which seems like an insurmountable task. I'm no longer able to do this on my own. I need You back in my life because I'm not strong enough. Keep me safe and forgive me for all of my sins. I know that I'm a mess, and that I've made so many mistakes, but I also think that You will forgive me.*

It wasn't a fancy prayer, but it was all she had at the moment. She put her head in her hands, closed her eyes and continued to ask God to help her.

When a hand landed on her shoulder, she jumped, then relaxed when she saw it was Rex. "Hi," she said softly. The truth was, she hadn't been completely alone. Rex had been here through it all. And thinking about what he meant to her made her afraid of feelings she didn't know if she could handle.

He took a seat beside her on the couch. "You look as if you could use a friend."

She blew out a breath. "That's an understatement."

"Anything you want to talk about?"

As she looked into his eyes, she felt safe. As if he was really on her side. "I was actually just praying. Can you believe that?"

"I can. God is waiting for you, Lily. He hasn't gone anywhere. Even when you may think you're all alone, drifting, He's right there. He's never left your side."

"I never thought I'd have a relationship with Him again." She honestly wasn't convinced He would accept her again after she'd turned her back on her faith. "Have you heard anything else from Eliza?"

He nodded. "I have. And it's really unbelievable.

The story only gets stranger with each piece of information I get."

That piqued her interest. "What did she say?"

"They finished the initial search of Sean's apartment." He paused and took a breath. "Are you sure you want to hear this now? We can talk later, once you get more rest."

"Absolutely. I may be having a weak moment, but knowledge is always better than being in the dark. I can't fight what I don't know."

Rex made direct eye contact with her. "Sean basically had a shrine to all of the victims in his apartment, including you."

A wave of apprehension washed over her. But she needed details to be able to assess the legitimacy of the threat. "Like what? What type of shrine?"

"Pictures. A lot of pictures all displayed on the wall. A wall completely devoted to all of the women he has killed, plus you. There were photos taken in a variety of situations. Some outside your house, some near that farmhouse you photographed, others at random stores or parks. He had pictures of the other victims, as well, going about their daily routines in various settings. The evidence strongly suggests that Sean Bishop is the serial killer we've be looking for."

"I never got even one inkling of that from any of my interactions with him. Not a single time did I feel that his interest was anything other than professional. If he really was the killer, wouldn't he have slipped up at some point? A weird reaction or an interest that seemed to be too much? There was none of that." Something felt so wrong about all of this to her.

"It does seem surprising. But I've had to keep reminding myself that sometimes the most skilled serial killers are able to compartmentalize so that he could act completely normal around you. It's one of the characteristics that separate serial killers from your run-of-the-mill murderers, and it's what makes them so dangerous."

"That still doesn't explain who attacked me at my house at the beginning of this nightmare. Sean was with you when you responded to the 911 call during the attack. Doesn't that loose end bother you?"

"It does concern me, but Eliza is focused like a laser beam on the accomplice-slash-hired-hand theory. And once Eliza has her mind set on something, there's no letting up until she gets where she wants to go. And she truly believes Sean is at the center of all of this."

"And what about Sean? Is he talking?"

"Nope. He's a police officer. He knows his rights. And he definitely understands the stakes of this are unbelievably high—being charged with six murders plus several counts of attempted murder. He immediately asked for an attorney, and I can't blame him. I'd do the exact same thing if I were arrested. I haven't heard what happened after he asked for a lawyer. Once lawyers get involved, it always gets complicated."

"My gut is just screaming at me that this is all wrong, Rex. Nothing about it makes sense."

"I feel the same way," he said. "But they are building a case with a lot of evidence against Sean. And I just don't know how all of the physical evidence could be wrong."

"There's such a thing as being framed." She couldn't hold back. She wanted to be able to talk openly with Rex. "I saw it happen multiple times while I was at the Agency."

"This would've had to have been a pretty elaborate setup. Not a simple feat."

"Well, we already know that our killer is highly skilled. I don't think it's outside the realm of possibility. I'm not planning to let my guard down."

"On that point we are in complete agreement. I'm not going to just leave you hanging until I'm completely satisfied this is over."

"What if the FBI has a different idea?"

"I'll do whatever it takes to keep you safe, Lily." He paused. "And Grace, too, of course."

She looked into his dark eyes and felt a warming in her heart. This man was standing by her side, and she treasured his loyalty. After James's betrayal, she never thought she'd trust again—herself or another man. While there would always be that bit of distrust that flowed through her because of what happened, deep in her heart she didn't think Rex would ever betray her. A mix of fear and hope flowed through her as she felt torn about the possibility of opening up her heart again.

"Sir." One of the FBI agents on security detail walked into the room. "I'm sorry to interrupt, but I thought you'd want to see this." The short and stocky blond agent walked over to the coffee table and got the remote to turn on the TV.

The Atlanta local evening news was on the screen. The agent turned up the volume. Lily watched as a gray-haired man in a dark, expensive-looking suit with a red-checkered tie was talking.

"My client, Officer Bishop, is completely innocent. It's ludicrous to accuse an Atlanta police officer with his impeccable record of committing these heinous crimes. I'm confident that once all the evidence is gathered, Sean Bishop will be fully exonerated."

"Thank you for that explanation, Mr. Webb," the pretty brunette newscaster said. "But are you actually insinuating that the FBI and Atlanta Police Department have gotten the wrong man? That your client is actually being falsely accused?" The reporter eyed him with skepticism, waiting for his reply.

"I'm not insinuating anything, ma'am. I'm straight out saying it." Mr. Webb leaned toward her in his chair. "Officer Sean Bishop is innocent. In a rush to find a suspect for these murders and try to calm down the local community, the FBI has completely overstepped its reach and gone after what they perceive as an easy target. Because Officer Bishop was working this case, and because he's only been on the Atlanta police force a relatively short amount of time, he made for a convenient suspect."

The anchor's dark eyes widened. "If your client is innocent, do you have the ability to clear his name?" The reporter was obviously trying to make a big headline. That was her job after all. But Lily was curious as to what the lawyer's response was going to be.

"Well, the FBI is trying to find a so-called accomplice because it is impossible that my client was involved with one of the attacks. I think that right there should send up a big red flag to people."

"I can understand your point."

"And I have to say something else that's very important for everyone out there watching tonight to understand."

"Sure, please go ahead," the reporter said.

"Since Officer Bishop is innocent, that means a serial killer is still out there in our community."

The reporter nodded. "I think we all need to remember that in our system one is innocent until proved guilty, and that it is always smart to be vigilant about one's own personal security." She looked back toward Mr. Webb. "Thank you for joining us tonight. We appreciate your time."

"Thanks for having me," Mr. Webb said.

The FBI agent turned down the volume on the TV and then looked at Rex. "Do you need anything, sir?"

"No, thank you. We're good."

The agent nodded and walked out of the living room.

"So what did you think of that?" Lily asked.

Rex rubbed his chin and sat in silence. After a long moment he responded, "I don't think you can put too much stock in an attorney's staunch defense of his client, but he raises the same concerns that you and I already had."

"But if they have the wrong man, that means the killer is out there, like Mr. Webb said. I'm not safe, and neither are the countless women he could target."

Lily wasn't exactly looking forward to meeting with Atlanta district attorney Steffie Hood, but she didn't really have much of a choice. And this would give her a way to size up the case against Sean and see how this was all going to unfold. Because Lily knew enough about the criminal justice system to understand that she would be a witness. And not just any witness but probably the star witness for the prosecution. That was basically the last thing she wanted. Not only because she didn't believe Sean was guilty, but she also didn't need that type of publicity.

She and Rex walked into the Fulton County district attorney's office in downtown Atlanta. Rex pushed the up button on the elevator. They were going to the fourth floor to meet in Steffie's office. From the limited intel gathering that Lily was able to do, it appeared that the district attorney had a reputation for being tough as nails.

"All you have to do is tell her the facts as you know them," Rex said. "You're not obligated to do any more than that."

"I'm not worried about any obligations, but you know it's going to be hard for me to not give my opinion. I'm going to be honest about how I feel."

The elevator bell rang, indicating they had reached the fourth floor.

"After you," he said.

She walked toward the receptionist's desk and asked for Steffie Hood. They were ushered into a small conference room with a round wooden table and told that Steffie would be in to see them soon.

A few minutes later, the door opened and district attorney Steffie Hood walked in, looking every part the seasoned prosecutor with her black briefcase in hand. She wore her dark hair pulled back in a tight bun. Steffie's black power suit was courtroom ready. This woman screamed *confidence* with every step she took.

Steffie's brown eyes were serious, and she immediately focused in on Lily.

"Ms. Parker, I'm Steffie Hood." The prosecutor reached out her perfectly manicured hand and gave Lily a firm shake. Steffie towered over Lily and had to be at least five foot eight or nine. Lily couldn't help but notice that Steffie also wore some serious black heels.

"Nice to meet you," Lily said. It was the polite thing to say even if Lily didn't really want any part of this. She still refused to believe that Sean was the killer, but for now she had to try to keep an open mind about what the prosecutor had to say.

"And I'm Rex Sullivan, FBI." Rex offered his hand as Steffie sized him up.

"Agent Sullivan, I think I'd prefer to speak with Ms. Parker alone." Steffie eyed Rex warily.

"I can speak completely freely in front of Rex," Lily told Steffie. "Since he responded to the initial

911 call he's been by my side every step of the way."
Lily refused to give Steffie the upper hand.

"I understand that, but you are both going to be
witnesses in this case against Officer Bishop, and I
prefer to talk to my witnesses individually. Agent Sullivan, you are welcome to wait in the reception area
and grab a cup of coffee while I talk to Ms. Parker."

Rex stood up and nodded. "Are you going to want
to talk to me today, too?"

Steffie looked down at her watch. "It depends on
how long I go with Ms. Parker."

"Understood." He looked toward Lily. "I'll be outside if you need anything."

"Ms. Parker will be completely safe here," Steffie
said. "I can assure you of that." It appeared she took
offense that Rex would presume there could be a potential threat in her presence.

Rex didn't respond to the DA's comment, but instead
exited the room quietly, leaving Lily alone with her.

"Please take a seat so we can get started," Steffie
said.

The sooner Lily told her story, the sooner they
could leave. "All right," Lily said.

Steffie opened up her briefcase and pulled out a
legal pad and pen. "I'm just going to take some notes
as we talk. I like to fully document these witness in-
terviews in real time to make sure I have an accurate
record of everything that's said. Not to mention it's
another reason I asked Rex to leave. It's better from a
legal perspective for me to get one person's full story
without having the other person being able to pipe in."

"That's fine," Lily replied. Unlike most people that Steffie probably dealt with, Lily wasn't intimidated by her.

"Why don't we start at the beginning," Steffie said.

"The first night I came into contact with the killer?" Lily asked. While she didn't want to necessarily be contentious with the prosecutor, she also wanted to fully vet her theories.

"Well, that's an interesting way to set it up. I don't know that I'd call it your first contact with the killer. I'd like to talk about the night you were attacked in your home. I'm particularly interested in that night because Officer Bishop could not have been at your house."

"You're right about that. There's no way that Officer Bishop was the man who attacked me. Don't you think that's an issue we need to deal with here?"

Steffie's lips drew down in a frown. "Ms. Parker, it's my job to worry about the implications of all of that. What I need from you is your side of the story so I can determine my legal strategies."

Lily recounted the entire ordeal in great detail from the night she was attacked at her home until the latest attempt on her life through the poisoning of her pizza. She didn't leave out anything, as she wanted to put it all on the table for the prosecutor.

Steffie took copious notes, filling up pages and pages of her legal pad. She asked very pointed questions but never once cut Lily off, allowing her to get out every detail of her story.

"This has been extremely helpful," Steffie said. "I

appreciate how thorough you've been in explaining everything that has happened to you."

"I want you to have all the facts."

"And I'm grateful for that. But now I've got a few tougher questions for you. I know I said I just wanted to hear your side of the story, but I'm going to tread in a dangerous area for us lawyers."

"Dangerous how?" Lily didn't trust this attorney to really get down to the truth, but her curiosity was piqued.

Steffie smiled. "I want to ask your opinion."

"My opinion on what?"

"As you've probably already surmised, I'm not the type of person to beat around the bush, Ms. Parker. So I'm just going ask you point-blank. Do you believe that Officer Bishop is the man who has made multiple attempts on your life?"

Without a second's hesitation, Lily responded, "No. I don't."

Steffie nodded but didn't write anything down. "And why is it you feel that way? And let me say, I want your honest, unfiltered opinion. Now is not the time to hold back on me or be diplomatic, because I want to understand your perspective. In fact, I need to understand."

Lily couldn't help but smile. The prosecutor didn't have to worry about Lily holding back. "There's no way Officer Bishop is your man. Some of my belief is based purely on gut instinct. There wasn't a single sign that he had any issue with me during the many encounters we had. He always conducted himself with complete professionalism, totally focused on his job as an APD officer. I would like to think that even a skilled killer couldn't keep up that type of ruse perfectly day in and day out. Particularly one who was dead set on killing me."

"The way you phrased your response, it seems like you have something else to say in addition to just your gut instincts."

Lily nodded. "It's all too neat. This entire thing wrapped up like a bow and delivered right to your doorstep. The shrine at Sean's house to all of his victims feels like a setup. And while it might not be a big deal to you that Sean has an alibi for the first attack against me, the overwhelming evidence on serial killers is that they work alone. All of the experts have said that. It would be entirely out of place for him to have hired someone to come after me initially and then take over himself after that. You'd have to agree with me on that."

"I'm just listening to what you have to say. I'm not here to argue my points right now. I'll save that for the courtroom."

"Well, that's my opinion, and just to be perfectly clear, if anyone else asks me what I think, I'll tell them the same exact thing. I believe the real killer is still out there."

"I completely understand your hesitation, but as a prosecutor my duty is to go where the clues take me. I simply can't turn my back on the mounting evidence against Officer Bishop. Not just the shrine at his home, but the DNA evidence found at one of the murder scenes he wasn't working. While you can argue that anything could be a setup, at some point the evidence speaks louder than any legal argument I could make."

"I understand your point, but it doesn't change my outlook. No disrespect to you as the prosecutor, but I'm the one literally living these events day in and day out."

"I'm not discounting that fact, but I think in a way you're letting your personal feelings for the man you thought you knew as an upstanding police officer get in the way of being completely objective. And just because all the pieces don't fit together in a perfect puzzle doesn't mean he's innocent. It just means my job is more difficult, but I'm not one to shy away from a challenge. Especially when the lives of innocent women are on the line."

"And you still plan on moving forward with Sean's prosecution?" Lily asked, although she already knew the answer. "Even after all I've said to you? If you put me on the stand I will say that I think Sean is innocent."

"I have a job to do here, Ms. Parker. While I certainly appreciate your opinion, at the end of the day, all prosecutorial decisions are mine. Our community has been terrorized by this killer, and the lives of six innocent women have been lost. The families want and deserve justice. The public expects a rapid and efficient prosecution. I plan to deliver."

"What does all of this mean for me?"

"It means you will be a witness at trial. Assuming this goes to trial and a plea deal isn't struck. The stakes are so high here, it's entirely possible we can come to a plea agreement. Of course Officer Bishop's lawyer is going to be out in the press vigorously defending him, but at the end of the day it's his job to save his client from the death penalty. A plea deal is the only way to ensure that will happen—and that's only if I decide I want to make that option available. A lot of people will want to see Officer Bishop put to death for the crimes he has committed."

"From the looks of it, I can't imagine Sean's lawyer ever advising him to take a deal."

Steffie raised an eyebrow. "You would be surprised what people will do when confronting the possibility of facing the death penalty."

Lily knew that Georgia still used the death penalty. And it greatly troubled her that an innocent man could be wrongly prosecuted and then put to death. She had to do something to stop that from happening. "You heard what I said, though. I'm not going to change my opinion. If you end up putting me on the witness stand, I'll repeat exactly what I've said here today."

"That's my problem to deal with, not yours."

"Seems to me that the jury would care about my opinion. Seeing as I've been the main target here."

Steffie rose from her seat. "I think we've accomplished more than enough for one day."

"You know, I have to say one more thing." Lily couldn't hold her tongue.

"Okay."

"I believe in the justice system. I know it doesn't

work perfectly, but I do believe in it. And someone in your role should think long and hard about prosecuting someone when there are serious doubts in place. You're potentially destroying an innocent man's life."

"Believe me, Ms. Parker, I take my job very seriously. And I've heard your feelings on the subject loud and clear. I'll walk you out."

Steffie had clearly ended the meeting even if Lily could've said a lot more. But Lily felt she had done her part by expressing her opinion. They walked out of the conference room and into the lobby area.

"Agent Sullivan, I'll call you to set up another time to talk."

"I'll wait to hear from you, then," Rex said.

"Thank you again, Ms. Parker." Steffie turned and walked away back down the hall.

"You were in there a long time," Rex said.

"Let's get out of here." Lily started walking to the elevator. "She's going after Sean full throttle. I don't think she really cares if he's actually the killer. I think she cares more about her career and putting away a serial killer to add a notch to her legal wins."

"I made some phone calls while I was waiting on you to finish up. Turns out that Steffie Hood has some serious political aspirations. She wants to use this job as a springboard to run for office. And what better résumé builder than putting away a heinous serial killer? It would make her a superstar in the community."

"It sickens me that she would put political ambition ahead of the lives of innocent people."

"Well, in her defense, maybe she has convinced herself that Sean is the killer."

"What really matters at the end of the day is that the real killer is still on the loose," Lily said. "And we have to find him before he strikes again."

NINE

Rex clenched his fists to keep from losing his cool. Eliza had come over to the safe house bringing news that he thought might come but that he definitely didn't want to hear. Now he and Eliza had to break it to Lily.

They found Lily in the living room watching TV, with Grace snuggled up by her side. The local news was on, and district attorney Steffie Hood was front and center on the screen. That prosecutor was really beginning to irk him. Rex didn't have to hear what she was saying to know. The Bureau had given him a heads-up. Steffie was moving forward with six counts of murder and multiple attempted-murder counts. She had also promised a speedy trial in which she would definitely seek the death penalty.

"You shouldn't watch that," Eliza told Lily.

Lily looked up at her. "I just can't help it. This woman has some nerve. Why ask my opinion about Sean's guilt if she had already decided to move forward regardless?"

"We actually need to talk to you about something else," Eliza said.

"What's wrong?" Lily asked with wide eyes. "Is there another body?"

"No, it's nothing like that," Rex said. "If anything, just the opposite."

Lily grabbed the remote from the coffee table and turned off the TV. "Just tell me what it is. I can handle it."

Eliza sat in the chair across from Lily, and Rex took a seat beside Lily on the couch. Rex looked at her, took a deep breath to steady his nerves. "The FBI has decided to accept the district attorney's position that Sean is the killer."

Lily looked as if she'd been slapped. "Even when we know there's no way the first attack could've been him?"

"Yes, everyone has theories on that, but it seems that a wire transfer was made from Sean's account to an untraceable offshore account. After uncovering that additional piece of information, the FBI is comfortable with the theory that he paid someone to attack you that night."

"So what does this mean for me?" Lily asked.

"As of tonight, the FBI is officially ending your security detail," Rex said. "The powers that be think that you're no longer in any danger. There's very strong evidence tying Sean to the crimes. To them, this is the end of the road because the killer is in custody and the threat is no longer present."

"I know this is very troubling," Eliza said. "But

with the FBI's limited resources, all efforts must be placed on active cases with live threats. And right now the evidence is not supporting that."

"I have to ask something. Do the two of you really believe that Sean's the killer? That they caught the right guy?" Lily asked.

"I've been somewhat skeptical of Sean's guilt mostly because I didn't want it to be him, even though I saw all the facts pointing that way. But this wire transfer really tipped the balance for me," Eliza said. "While we spend a tremendous amount of time working on profiles and understanding the psychology of a killer, it's also true that there are times when the killer doesn't act in a way that fits neatly into one of our established profiles. People are unique and we learn more and more about the psychology of a serial killer with each new case."

"And what about you?" Lily looked at him expectantly.

"I hear everything that Eliza and my FBI colleagues have said, but I can't help the feeling that Sean is not our man. Even more troubling is the possible fallout if we're wrong about this. Your life being on the line, for one. Not to mention the likelihood that the killer is still at large." Unable to contain his nervous energy, Rex stood and started pacing back and forth as he spoke. "But the FBI's position is that the evidence against Sean is so strong that to divert resources would be wasteful."

"What does the APD think?" Lily asked.

"Well, Derrick is still defending Sean, even though

he's having a hard time doing it publicly because he was basically told by his boss to keep his mouth shut and let the justice system handle it." Rex shifted his weight from one foot to the other. "Then there are those at the force who have fallen in line and think that Sean is guilty."

"So the bottom line is that I'm on my own from here on out," Lily said.

As he looked at her, he didn't see an ounce of fear. Just pure determination. One of the many things that had drawn him to her was how strong she was in the face of danger. "No, Lily. You're most definitely not on your own, because you have me."

She shook her head. "You can't just stop your investigative work to babysit me. There are plenty of cases that could use your expertise."

Eliza's phone rang loudly. "I'm sorry, I have to take this. I have a meeting with a victim from another case, so I should go." She walked over to Lily and knelt down beside her. "I know you're going to be okay, but if you ever need a friend to talk to about all of this, please call me." Then Eliza looked toward Rex. "Take care of her. I'll touch base with you tomorrow." With that, she exited the room.

Lily motioned toward him. "Come over here and sit down, Rex. Your pacing is making me nervous."

The last thing he wanted to do was stress her out further. Although she seemed to be handling the news much better than he had. He'd promised himself that he wasn't going to let anything happen to this woman, and he wouldn't abandon her now.

"Talk to me," she said.

He sat down beside her and looked into her eyes. "I am not going to cut and run, Lily. It's just not who I am."

She reached out and grabbed his hand. "Rex, please do not feel any sort of duty to protect me. You've gone above and beyond time and time again. I promise you that I can take care of myself. I've been doing it for years."

Before he could stop himself, he reached out and gently cupped her cheek. "This goes so far beyond duty or the obligations I have as an FBI agent, Lily."

"What do you mean?"

"Because somewhere on this crazy journey, I've started to develop feelings for you."

He realized his mistake as she moved back from his touch. Too much, too fast.

"Rex, I value your friendship and all you've done for me, but I don't know that I can give you what you're looking for. Don't you want to find someone without all of my baggage?"

"You're way too hard on yourself, Lily. You deserve a chance at happiness. We all do." Yeah, he'd waited years after his heart was broken to really consider getting close to another woman, but he firmly believed that there was something special between him and Lily.

"I'm afraid that I won't ever be able to fully open up my heart again." She paused. "Even if I want to try."

"You've experienced tremendous hurt and loss, but you shouldn't have to be alone forever because of it."

Her eyes glittered with unshed tears. "Some people are just meant to be alone. I can't risk my heart again, Rex. I'm sorry."

He wasn't planning on giving up, but he realized he'd pushed her far enough for now. He'd retreat a couple of steps, but he knew his feelings for her weren't going anywhere. "I respect that, but that still doesn't change my stance on your security. I'm not letting you go out there alone. Not when there's still a chance the real killer is walking the streets."

"So what is your plan? I don't have anyplace to stay because of the fire."

"You and Grace can stay at my house. I have a guest room and plenty of space. That way I know you'll be safe."

"I know you're just trying to be helpful, but what if this isn't necessary? What if you and I got it wrong and everyone else is right? What if Sean is guilty, and I can go about living my normal life?"

He reached out and grabbed her hand again. "Look me in the eyes, Lily, and tell me that you truly believe that. That you think Sean is the man who has tried to kill you and has brutally murdered six other women."

She looked away and then back at him. "You know I can't say that."

"Then, it's settled. We'll pack up and go to my place. Derrick has also volunteered to help us in any way we need."

"And what about your job?"

"I have more vacation time built up than you can imagine. Today I told my boss that I would be using it."

"Why?"

"Because you're worth it." He planned to show her just how much she meant to him.

As Lily had looked into Rex's brown eyes earlier and heard him tell her that he had feelings for her, it was as if the world had shaken underneath her.

Because if she was being honest, she'd developed feelings for him, too. Strong feelings, at that. But it was far too dangerous for her to act on them. For one, she was still being hunted by a serial killer. Even if all of law enforcement and the district attorney thought that Sean was guilty, she knew better.

But beyond the current threat, the even bigger threat to her was an emotional one. Of allowing herself to be vulnerable again. To open her heart to a man. She'd done it only once before and the ramifications had been life altering. Not only had she been betrayed, but James's duplicity had forced her to take his life. Even though she knew she'd had no choice, that it was either kill or be killed. She'd been struggling to pick up the pieces ever since.

Yeah, she knew there was no comparing the two men. James and Rex couldn't have been more different. But her heart was still going to hold her back. It was still telling her that there was no one worth risking that kind of pain ever again. A pain that felt like a punch to the gut every single day. A pain that she relived with each new breath she took. Even with the passage of time, her wounds still felt raw. A gnawing ache that never went away.

"Hey," Rex said. He walked into the kitchen carrying the groceries that they had picked up on the way to his house. "Just sit tight and I promise dinner will be great."

"I didn't realize you had culinary skills. I can't wait to see what you cook up."

He smiled as he starting pulling the groceries out of the bags. "There's a lot you don't know about me, Lily."

She knew this man cared for her. It was evident by the look of concern in his eyes even as he smiled. But she also knew she needed to keep their relationship strictly platonic. That was the way it had to be. Right? Because what if she did start acting on her feelings and then got hurt again…? Or, even worse, what if she hurt him, even if she didn't intend to?

"So what's for dinner?" she asked.

"My special pasta recipe with grilled chicken."

"Sounds delicious. I'm not much of a cook myself."

"I started cooking once I graduated college. I figured if I was going to be on my own I needed to learn how to do more than get takeout every night."

She laughed. "I'm much more in the takeout category myself."

"Your CIA lifestyle didn't exactly lend itself to culinary expansion."

"You're right about that. One of the many sacrifices I made to be in the CIA."

He started chopping vegetables with a quick hand and looked up at her as he stopped for a second. "And I know you want your space, but until I have a better handle on the situation, I'm not letting you out of my sight."

She sighed, knowing there was no point in arguing with him. "You're a stubborn man. Did you know that?"

He laughed loudly. "I have been told that a time or two."

"Seriously, I do have a question for you."

"Shoot," he said, as he turned on the stove.

"How long are we going to do this? I get that things are uncertain right now, but we can't live like this forever. We both need to get back to our lives."

"You're really anxious to get rid of me, huh? Am I that bad?"

"I'm being serious here, Rex. Being constantly on edge and on guard isn't a healthy way for either of us to live."

He nodded. "Okay. Well, I think time will reveal all we need to know. If Sean is truly the killer, then you should be safe with him in custody. That means that nothing should happen to you from here on out. And if the killer is still out there, it's only a matter of time before he strikes again. So I'm not willing to put a deadline on the situation right now."

"They are going to start the repairs to my house on Monday, but that might take some time. I'd be happy to stay with Alison, but not until I know I wouldn't be putting her in danger."

"That makes sense. I promise I'll give you space. This house is plenty big for the two of us and Grace."

As she looked into his eyes, she wondered if that was true. She knew she had to protect her body from the killer—but was her heart safe from Rex?

A few days passed with no new threats and Lily started to consider the distinct possibility that Sean was guilty. That he had really planned on having her taken from her house, tortured and killed. All part of his deadly path that included taking the lives of numerous other innocent women. A police officer, someone who had sworn to protect and defend, had violated his oath.

She felt a strange combination of relief and disappointment. They'd dropped Grace off at Derrick's, and he would take her for a late-night run with a couple of his training officers. Now she and Rex were on the way back to his house.

She was starting to get antsy being around Rex so much. Thankfully, he hadn't brought up his feelings for her again. But she had her own feelings to rein in. Rex was genuinely a great man. Not only was he handsome and smart, he lived out his faith through his actions. He was loyal and protective of those he cared for. Her respect only grew for him by the day. But she knew it was a lot more than respect she was starting to feel for him. Her heart was involved now, and she didn't know exactly what to do about it.

"Anything you need before we head back to the house?" Rex asked.

"Nothing I need, but I could really go for some greasy food right now."

He laughed. "What, have I been cooking too healthy for you?"

"I don't mean to sound ungrateful." She looked over at him. Gone were the tense shoulders and furrowed brow that had been his trademark since the beginning of their time together. He was finally starting to relax. She thought they were both beginning to realize they may have been wrong about Sean. And that everything was going to be okay after all. If all went as planned, she'd be getting back to her photography business soon.

"No, I get it. What kind of greasy food are you looking for? Something like burgers and fries? I know you said you didn't want pizza again for a while and that's totally normal after what had happened."

"Yeah, poisoning will do that to a person." As they exited the Atlanta highway and turned onto one of the side streets, she found herself actually thanking God. Just for being alive. Having more opportunity to live and do something meaningful with her life.

"Then, cheeseburgers and greasy fries it is."

"Awesome. Thank you." She looked over at Rex, expecting him to be smiling, but he wasn't. In fact, he had a big frown on his face, the first she'd seen in days.

Then she saw that his eyes were glued to the rearview mirror. She turned around to see what had captured his attention. "What is it?"

"Probably nothing, but just being cautious."

"You're not looking as if it's nothing." Just as the words came out of her mouth, he floored it, throwing her off balance. Thankfully, she had a seat belt on.

"Hang on," he said, his voice strained.

She braced herself, but couldn't help but look back again. That was when she saw the large, dark SUV gaining on them. The headlights were bright and barreling down on them.

"That isn't just an aggressive driver, is it?"

"I don't think so. Let me speed up to see what happens."

"How much power does your Jeep have?"

"Enough. Especially with me driving." He punched the accelerator and put some distance between them and the SUV.

She took a few deep breaths to steady herself. This wasn't her first car chase. She'd been involved in a few nasty ones during her time at the CIA. But she preferred to be behind the wheel. Having no choice now, she relinquished total control to Rex.

He kept up the furious pace, but the SUV was gaining on them.

Suddenly, she was thrown forward when the other car rammed them in the rear. "This isn't just fun and games. He's trying to hurt us."

"Agreed. I'm going to pull a fast turn when I find the perfect street, so be prepared. He still might hit us."

"I have my Glock. Please let me take a shot. If he's driving solo, he can't get to me."

"It's too risky."

Disabling the SUV would be their best chance to get away from this guy. She knew the area of town they were in now and there weren't going to be good options for taking a quick turn. "I'm sorry, Rex. I'm going to have to take action on this one. I promise I know what I'm doing."

She saw him visibly tense as he gripped the wheel even more tightly. "I can see that I can't talk you out of this."

"No. Just let me take a shot. It might get him off our tail."

"All right. But I can't slow down too much or we'll suffer a direct hit."

"I've got this, Rex. This isn't my first rodeo." Her statement put the smallest of smiles on his face. She pulled her Glock out of her purse and unfastened her seat belt.

"If you can't get a clear shot, get back in as quick as possible."

"Roger that," she said. In that moment, as pure adrenaline surged through her body, she realized there was a part of her that missed the feeling of being in the field. She rolled down the window and positioned herself where the SUV was in her direct line of sight. She could shoot left-handed if she needed to, but she was more precise with her right.

Lord, if You're still listening to my prayers, I could use Your help right now. Her hand steady and her aim solid, she took the shot. The glass of the front windshield of the SUV shattered. The bullet hit the passenger side, which was exactly where she'd aimed.

Unlike the killer, she wasn't trying to murder—just destabilize. And that was enough to get the result she wanted.

The driver of the SUV slammed on the brakes. Mission accomplished.

Not wasting any time, she slid back into the passenger seat and fastened her seat belt. Her heart raced, but it was well worth it.

"Good job, Lily. That was impressive."

"I told you I was a good shot."

She looked back and didn't see any sign of the SUV.

Finally able to let out a breath, she gathered her thoughts. "What are we going to do?"

"Sorry, Lily, the burger and fries will have to wait. We're going to head back to the house, and I'm going to start making calls."

"You don't think that was a random attack, do you?"

"Of course not. And neither do you. Either the hired gun is still coming after you, or it's a much worse alternative."

"What is that?"

"The real killer is on the hunt, and he won't stop until you're dead."

TEN

A man of his word, Rex made plenty of calls once they had gotten back to his house. Currently he was being joined in his kitchen by Derrick and Eliza, with two other FBI agents standing temporary guard outside. Lily was also there, refusing to be left out of the loop. And he couldn't blame her. This wasn't the time to cut her out.

"We can't get ahead of ourselves," Eliza said. "There is still a possibility that this attack had absolutely nothing to do with the serial killer. This is Atlanta. You were in an area that has a good amount of crime. It's not unheard of for things like this to happen."

"Eliza," Rex said, refusing to hold back. "I'm beginning to think that unless you're face-to-face with Lily's dead body, nothing is going to make you think this killer is still out there."

Eliza physically recoiled in her seat, eyes wide. She frowned. "Rex, you can't believe that's true."

"Rex, don't take this out on her," Lily said. "She's just trying to be objective here."

"Everyone needs to start looking at this entire situation from a logical perspective," Rex said. "No one really thought that Sean was capable of this to begin with. But because of the supposedly solid evidence, everyone rushed to judgment and wanted a quick trial and guilty verdict. But I don't see how we can ignore the facts right in front of us. It is much more likely that Sean is not our man. And if the real killer did come after Lily tonight, I wouldn't be surprised if another dead body turned up soon. This guy will only be able to suppress his emotional impulse to kill for so long." He was done biting his tongue and being a team player. If his FBI counterparts wanted to stick their heads in the sand, he had to be the one to open their eyes.

"That still doesn't explain away all the evidence we do have against Sean," Eliza said.

"But evidence can be planted and fabricated. Someone skilled with computers could've set up that wire transfer. That's just one example. The shrine to the victims at his place could've been planted there at the time when the killer knew the police and FBI would be searching it. It's not outside the realm of possibility that the killer had a master setup plan to frame Sean from the beginning."

"I agree with Lily," Derrick said. "I know I'm biased because Sean is one of my men, but I've always said that I didn't think he was the one. We can't start coming up with illogical scenarios to explain away what happened to Lily and Rex tonight. The chance of that being a random attack is remote at best."

Rex could see that Eliza still wasn't totally on board. And the fact was that he needed her solid support to make a case to the FBI that the full security team needed to be put back in place. And that the case was far from closed. "Eliza, what additional proof do you need?"

"I'm just trying to figure out how this all fits together," Eliza responded. "I do admit that this latest attack on you can't be discounted. There's always a risk that Sean was framed, even though I think it's a small one. So in this case, Rex, I'll go to bat for you to try to obtain additional FBI security. It doesn't matter if my opinion ultimately remains unchanged." Eliza shifted her focus toward Lily. "Because, frankly, I'm not willing to risk your life. I don't care about my ego in this."

"Good. I appreciate any backup I can get with the FBI higher-ups," Rex said. Having Eliza's support would definitely strengthen his cause.

"I am also looping in Steffie Hood. She should know about this," Eliza said.

Lily scoffed. "Believe me, there's nothing you could say to change that woman's mind. She's going full steam ahead with Sean's prosecution."

"Well, regardless, I plan on giving her a complete report. What she does with the information is on her and the DA's office." Eliza stood up. "I'm going to get out of here and start making phone calls. Including the one to your boss, Rex. I'll circle back around with you."

"And since you're my ride, I'm out of here, too,"

Derrick said. "If there's anything I can do from the APD side, I'm here."

"Thanks. We have the two FBI agents providing security for the night while my boss considers his next move," Rex said. "So we should be fine here."

With that, Eliza and Derrick walked out of the kitchen, leaving Rex alone with Lily. He stifled the urge to reach out and wrap his arms around her. "What are you thinking?" he asked.

"I think this latest incident is solid proof that Sean is innocent. I just don't buy the argument that we were a victim of random Atlanta road rage."

"We're both on the same page."

Grace barked loudly.

"I'm glad she wasn't in the car with us tonight," Lily said.

The truth was, Grace and Lily had both taken up residence in his heart. It was getting more and more difficult to imagine life without them. "Me, too."

"She seems to have really adjusted well to your place," she said.

"Yeah, she has." He had to hold back saying what he truly felt. That he wanted Lily to be adjusted to his place, too. Would a relationship with this woman be possible? It was certainly something he was praying for. He didn't want to push the issue, especially during such a dangerous and stressful time. But once this killer was put away, Rex intended to ask Lily on a proper date.

"So we wait to hear what the FBI does before we make our next move?" Lily asked.

"Yes." Tired of fighting his impulse to touch her, he reached out and took her hand in his. "You were great out there tonight. In addition to the stellar shot, you never lost your cool."

She smiled. "We make a good team."

"Yes, we do." Dare he take a chance and say something again about his feelings for her that kept getting stronger by the day?

"What is it?" Lily asked. "You're looking at me strangely."

He considered his words carefully as he looked into her eyes. There was so much he wanted to say, but mere words didn't seem to cut it at the moment.

He slowly leaned in toward her and reached out to touch her cheek. Then he brushed his lips gently against hers, only allowing himself to linger a moment. He pulled back and looked into her bright blue eyes, which were wide with surprise.

She didn't say a word, but there was something in the way she looked at him that made him think she felt something for him, too. The kiss had been brief, but it had told him everything he needed to know.

The next morning, Lily stood in the living room and was still reeling from Rex's kiss. It had only lasted a second, but it had been filled with so much promise, making it even harder for her to process her own feelings. She was scared of how attached she was becoming to Rex. And that kiss solidified what she had already feared—she was falling for this man.

"What's the latest news?" she asked Rex when he entered the room.

"APD is doing the best they can with the information we gave them on the SUV, but without a license plate, it's pretty much impossible to try to track down a car fitting its description in the city of Atlanta. It's like a needle in a haystack."

"I hear you." She took a seat on the couch. "My mind is in overdrive right now. Especially since I'm basically confined to the house. I just hate feeling so helpless."

"I'm sorry about having to stay in the house, but it's the safest thing for you to do right now while we're so uncertain about the situation."

"I appreciate you allowing us to stay here."

"Don't even think another thought about that. I wouldn't have it any other way."

"You have a nice neighborhood. It seems like a great place to live."

"I enjoy it. But honestly, I spend so little time at home I find it doesn't really matter if I have nice neighbors or not."

She nodded. "I get the whole being-married-to-the-job thing. I don't think it's a very good way to live, but I haven't had any success trying to break away from that. Even now with my photography, I throw myself into my work. My friends are always trying to get me to do more things, and I probably should make a bigger effort to be social."

"Yeah, a lot of us in the FBI probably have a very

bad work-life balance. But at least I'm not in denial about it."

"One day you may change your mind. You'll want more out of life. A family, a dog, the whole nine yards." Had she really just said that?

"You're right. I've just been enjoying the work so much that it doesn't feel as though I'm missing out."

"I totally get it."

"How has the transition been from CIA agent to photographer?"

Grace hopped up onto the sofa beside her and Lily was grateful for the distraction. "It's interesting that you use the word *transition* because that's exactly how it feels. It was kind of strange to come home and try to reconnect with my friends from childhood. I was worried that they'd be too different, or that they wouldn't want anything to do with me because I'd been completely AWOL since college."

"But they greeted you with open arms?"

"Yes. Especially Alison and Jackson. Guy gave me a bit of a harder time about being so disconnected, but as you know it isn't as if I could tell them what I'd been doing. It was better for them to think I was just being selfish and self-involved as opposed to knowing the truth."

"Maybe one day years from now, when it's safer, you'll be able tell them about your CIA career."

She laughed. "I can't even imagine what they'd say. I think they'd be shocked."

"Yeah. It's not every day that you find out one of your friends had been a spy."

"Hopefully, one day they'll know the true me without all the secrets. That would be nice. I think Alison would be a bit hurt, but I know they'd all appreciate that I took an oath to defend this country."

"Of course. You're fortunate to have friends you can trust." His phone rang and he pulled it out of his pocket. "I need to take this call."

As she watched him, his expression turned serious. His brow furrowed as he spoke into the phone. *Now what?* she thought. She really could use some good news after all of the bad things that had happened. But she had the feeling this wasn't going to be the news she wanted.

He ended the call. "That was Steffie Hood."

"Ugh," she said. "What does she want now?"

"She needs to see you at her office."

"Right now?"

"Yes. She said the sooner the better and that there's a time-sensitive issue she'd like to discuss with you in person. She was insistent. I think there might be a break in the case, Lily. But she was tight-lipped so I have no idea what it is."

"Then, I guess we have no choice but to go." She stood up from the couch. "Let's get going. I'd like to get this over with."

Lily didn't relish being summoned to Steffie Hood's office once again. What did the prosecutor want with her now? To try to convince her to change her testimony? That certainly wasn't going to happen.

"I'm only coming here because you told me I had to," Lily said to Rex.

They took the now-familiar path up to the fourth floor, where Steffie was actually waiting in the reception area to greet them.

Today the prosecutor wore her dark hair down and had on tortoiseshell reading glasses. Her impeccably tailored gray pantsuit looked more expensive than what one would expect she could afford on a prosecutor's salary. But that was really none of Lily's business.

"Ms. Parker, thank you for coming in again on such short notice. Please follow me into the conference room."

The fact that Steffie didn't even acknowledge Rex wasn't lost on Lily, but the other woman didn't object when Rex walked with them into the conference room.

"Have a seat," Steffie said. She also sat at the table, across from Lily.

"What is this all about?" Lily asked. Better to just get on with it.

"I actually have some news, and I wanted to share it with you personally before the inevitable media circus breaks out."

Lily realized she was gripping her chair for dear life. "What is it?"

"Yesterday Officer Bishop provided a full confession."

Lily felt her eyes widen. "What?"

Rex stood from his chair. "Yes, what do you mean?"

"Everyone just take a deep breath and calm down," Steffie said. "I'll explain everything that I can."

Lily's mind flooded with thoughts. How could this be possible? Hadn't Sean's lawyer just been out there adamantly defending him on the news? What could have possibly changed? What could've made Sean confess?

"Lily, I know, based on our previous discussions, that you had serious reservations about Sean being the killer. I wanted us to meet again face-to-face, given the latest turn of events."

Lily's heart thumped wildly as she prepared herself. "I'll listen to whatever it is you have to say."

"First, I want to make clear that this confession was one hundred percent voluntary."

Rex was now pacing the room. "And how do we know that?" he asked, raking his fingers through his hair. "You've been on the hunt to get Sean from the moment he was arrested."

Steffie let out a sigh and looked at Rex over wire-framed glasses. "Agent Sullivan, I'd appreciate it if you kept your commentary to yourself. If you can't, then I'd kindly ask you to let me speak with Ms. Parker privately."

Rex didn't respond but crossed his arms over his chest and slumped back into his chair. Lily could tell that he was trying to hold his tongue.

"Please continue," Lily said. She wanted to hear this story for herself and then make a determination.

"As I was saying." Steffie looked down and back up at Lily. "Officer Bishop actually asked for a meeting with me. He fired his defense counsel, and I assumed he was going to ask me to recommend a public defender or something. But that wasn't it at all."

"What exactly did he say?" Lily asked.

"He said he wanted to make a deal. If I took the death penalty off the table, he would provide information about all of the murders. I told him that if his statement satisfied me I would do as he asked."

Lily sat back and took it all in, but she couldn't believe what she was hearing.

"Then he point-blank said he wanted to confess to all of the killings. As you can imagine, this took me a bit by surprise." She paused. "At that time Officer Bishop proceeded to provide details of exactly what happened with each of his victims."

"How is that possible?" Lily asked more to herself than to Steffie.

"It's possible because he is the killer, Ms. Parker. If I had any doubts before, those have been put to rest after hearing him discuss in great detail how he killed these women. It was literally one of the most disturbing confessions I've ever heard."

"How was his demeanor?" Rex asked.

"He was very calm. Calculating even. I stared into the eyes of a cold-blooded killer. He showed no remorse. Not one ounce. But he said he wanted to confess because of you, Lily."

"Me? That doesn't make any sense."

"I'm just conveying what he told me. He said that he was doing it for you." Steffie reached out and grabbed Lily's hands. "I get the sense that you don't like me very much, Lily. And I'm perfectly fine with that. But you need to know that this nightmare is over. It's really finished. He won't be able to hurt you or other innocent women ever again. He will spend the rest of his life in prison for what he's done."

"What about the attack at my house? Did he say who was responsible for that? And the recent incident on the road?"

"Well, he didn't provide a name yet, but he did say that he paid off a hired gun for both of those attacks. The same guy. He also confirmed the wire transfer information. APD is working on tracking down his accomplice based on the intel we've gathered so far."

"And what else did he say?"

"Officer Bishop explained to me that he saw you out one day taking photographs in the park while he was on patrol and instantly was drawn to you. You were perfect in his mind because you already fit his victim profile. He'd already started down this deadly path."

"Then what happened?"

"He deviated a bit from his regular plan in that he hired someone to kidnap you from your house as an experiment. But after the guy failed to capture you, Sean realized that if he wanted it done right, he'd need to do most of the dirty work himself. It annoyed him that you got away, so he was intent on finishing the job. But he had a fail-safe in place in case he ever got caught, which explains the attack by the SUV."

Lily blew out a breath. These revelations were shaking her down to the core. She pictured Sean's face and tried to imagine him wanting to kill her. "This keeps getting stranger and stranger."

"I'm sorry, Lily. I know it's not what you expected to hear. But I'm trying to tell you everything that I can so that you can process this information and start getting your life back."

"And you're certain about all of this?" Lily asked.

Steffie nodded her head vigorously. "Absolutely. He disclosed details only the killer could know."

"It seems so wrong," Lily said softly.

"When you're dealing with criminals, sometimes they are unpredictable," Steffie said. "What is vitally important is that we can close this case and put this awful chapter behind us. The families can finally receive closure knowing that he will spend his life in prison for the heinous crimes he committed."

Lily sat back in her chair, head spinning. So many different emotions flowed through her. Could this really be true? Could it all be over? "Honestly, I just don't know what to say," Lily responded.

"It's a lot for you to handle, I realize that," Steffie said. "But once you start fully comprehending it all, you will feel better in the end because you can begin to heal."

Rex sat uncharacteristically quiet in his chair. She wondered what he was thinking, but she didn't want to have a conversation with him about it in front of Steffie.

"So what do we do now?" Lily asked.

"The confession will be hitting the news today. I'm sure this is going to be a 24/7 media event. I suspect a lot of people will be surprised by the outcome. While the details haven't been worked out, I can't imagine we'd take this to trial. There will probably be a formal plea deal worked out now that we have the confession. I told him I would take death off the table, and I'm staying true to my word. So you won't have to worry about testifying or anything like that."

"As far as you're concerned, I'm done with all of this?"

Steffie smiled. "Yes. And that should make you both relieved and happy. It's okay to be happy that this is over. It's been a terribly traumatic process for you."

Lily nodded, still feeling kind of cold inside.

"If you want to take a moment in here, that's fine. If you need anything else at all, just let me know." Steffie stood up and walked over to Lily, shaking her hand before leaving Lily and Rex alone in the conference room.

"Wow," Lily said. "Talk about being thrown for a loop." She pushed herself back from the table but remained seated.

Rex stood up and walked around the table to take a seat beside her. "Are you all right?" he asked gently.

"Yes, but honestly, I think I'm in a bit of shock."

"You're not the only one." He reached out and touched her shoulder. "But I guess it's like what Steffie said, sometimes criminals go outside profiles and MOs."

"But why confess, Rex? Why go through all of this, start fighting the case and then do a total about-face? Nothing about any of this fits together the way it should."

"Maybe there is still a shred of decency left in that man and he had a guilty conscience and wanted to let it all out. I'm also sure they're going to make him undergo psychological testing. The bottom line is that it looks as if Sean really did kill all those women, and he wanted to kill you, too."

That thought sent a wave of nausea over her. "That doesn't make me feel any better."

"I'm just trying to connect all the dots here. If we take everything presented as true, then you would no longer be in danger."

She looked directly into his eyes. "Do you have any concerns about this at all?"

"When it comes to your safety, Lily, I am always going to be extracautious."

"What does that mean in practice?"

"It means that until I'm absolutely sure there is no threat against you, I'm going to keep you safe."

"You don't have to do that."

"I know I don't have to, Lily, but I want to. I'll feel better knowing you're with me. I've already taken the vacation time. Let's just ride this out. I'd at least like to make sure they catch the accomplice. It would let me sleep better at night. Then we can talk about how to move forward."

She nodded as she sat there quietly and wondered what moving forward would even look like.

ELEVEN

"You're awfully quiet," Rex said. He looked across the kitchen table at Lily, who had just finished breakfast. In the few days since Sean had provided a full confession, there had been no threats against her of any kind. But his need to protect her had only grown stronger. Ever since he'd kissed her, he couldn't help but want a real relationship with her. But she had been keeping a safe distance from him. The wall wouldn't be apparent to those on the outside, but to him, it was palpable. It hurt him to have to entertain the idea that maybe she didn't feel the same way about him as he felt about her.

"We should talk," Lily said.

"Uh-oh." He couldn't help but smile.

"According to Derrick, they have the identity of the hired gun. APD has a BOLO out on him. We should be realistic. There's no way that guy is going to come anywhere near me."

"We don't know that for sure," Rex said. He could

tell where Lily was going with this. She was seeking an out. Specifically, to get away from him.

"I appreciate all you've done for me, Rex. Really, I do. But don't you think it's time for us to try to move on with our lives? Stop looking over our shoulders all the time? I spoke with Alison and she has her guest room all ready for me."

"I would feel a lot better once the suspect was in custody."

"That may never happen, though. He could be out of the country for all we know. I can't continue to just stay here under your watchful eye around the clock." She paused. "And you need to get back to work. To catching serial killers. That's your calling."

"I didn't do too well on this case, did I?" She'd hit him in a sensitive spot. He still couldn't get over the fact that he'd been completely blind to Sean's guilt. He's spent a lot of time with the guy, and not once had it ever occurred to Rex that Sean should've been on his list of suspects.

"Rex, absolutely no one suspected that Sean was the killer. And everyone agrees this is a rare case."

He shook his head. "But how can I call myself an expert if I don't catch on to the rare cases, Lily? That's exactly what I'm supposed to be able to do. Crack the cases that no one else can." He hadn't planned on getting this emotional, but all of a sudden he couldn't hold back anymore. It felt better to let it out.

Lily reached across the table and took his hands. He felt a stirring deep inside when she touched him.

"Rex, listen to me," she said. "You cannot put this

type of blame on yourself. The only one responsible for these crimes is Sean. Not you, not me, not anyone else. It's on him."

"I don't see it that way."

"All the more reason you need to move on with your life and get back to work. I hope you don't take this the wrong way, but you've lost perspective. This case has gotten inside your head."

She was completely right, and one of the reasons he'd lost perspective was because of the woman who was sitting in front of him. "You're right. Which is why I'm going to take a leave of absence from the FBI."

"What?" she asked loudly. "No. You can't do that. Not because of this case."

He'd rarely seen her so worked up. "I've made my decision. So regardless of whether you leave or not, I'm not going back to the FBI right now."

"What will you do?"

"I'm not sure," he said softly. "I need some time to reevaluate. To rethink things and try to get some perspective again."

"Rex, is this about more than just the case?"

"It's predominantly about the case."

"And what else?"

"My instincts seem to be wrong about everything lately," he said quietly. "Starting with the case."

"And ending with?"

"You, Lily."

Her eyes widened. "How so?"

"I care for you, Lily. A lot. And you obviously

don't feel the same way. I thought you were starting to have feelings, too, but I can see now I was also wrong about that. I'm not going to lie. It really hurts to come to that realization, but now that I have, it's just time for me to move on. To face reality. To accept the fact I'm going to have to let you go."

She pulled her hands away from his, leaving him cold. "It's not like that, Rex."

"Then, how is it?"

"I never said that I didn't want to be with you. I said I didn't know if I could be with you. And I care about you a lot, too."

"Fine," he said. "Are you going to say that I'm wrong, and that you actually do have romantic feelings for me?"

"It's complicated."

"Is it?" To him it wasn't the least bit complicated.

"There's too much at stake, Rex. I already told you before that I just don't know if I can go down that road again after what happened with James. I still feel a combination of numbness and pain from the ordeal. I wouldn't want anyone to have to deal with that baggage. And especially not a man like you. You deserve better than that. You deserve better than me. Than what I could ever offer you."

He couldn't believe the words that were coming out of Lily's mouth. "You can't really think that. That I'm too good for you? No, Lily, if anything, it's the other way around."

She hung her head. "You're amazing, and I am thoroughly damaged."

This time he reached out and grabbed her hands. "Why don't you let me decide what I need? And what I need is you."

"Rex," she whispered. As he looked into her bright blue eyes, they started to fill ever so slightly with tears. She got up from the table and walked into the other room.

He slumped down in his chair. He was certain he'd seen something in her eyes. She wouldn't have gotten upset if she didn't have feelings for him. Now that he'd caught a glimpse of what was in her heart, he wasn't going to give up on what they could have together.

One week later, Lily was miserable. She hated to admit to herself that she actually missed Rex. A lot. More than she'd ever missed anyone before.

But as much as it hurt her, she was still keeping a safe distance. Because even if she did really care for Rex, she knew that things would eventually end badly. Probably all because of her and her emotional walls that seemed to be more like insurmountable towers at this point. She would just have to take the short-term hurt instead of the long-term, which would inevitably be much worse. But her heart felt as though it was being torn in two.

While her house was being renovated, Alison had taken her in, like any good friend would. Now she was waiting for Jackson to pick her up for dinner. Alison had a business dinner to attend and didn't want Lily to be alone, even though Lily had insisted she would be fine. But Jackson offered to step in, and Lily thought it would be nice to spend time with him and catch up. Try to get back to normal. Or at least as normal as things could ever be again.

When she saw him pull up in his blue pickup truck, she smiled. "Bye, Grace. You be good while I'm at dinner with Jackson." She gave her dog a pat and a quick kiss on the head and locked up Alison's house.

"Hey," she said. She walked down the front porch steps to meet him.

He gave her a quick hug. "I hope you're hungry, because I'm starving."

"Me, too. Where are we going?"

"Believe it or not, I'm cooking."

She laughed. "Where is Jackson and what did you do with him? Since when in the world did you start cooking?"

"I've learned a lot over the years, Lily." He looked down at her and smiled.

"Well, if you're cooking, then I'm eating. Because you know very well that I can't cook anything unless it involves pressing the buttons on the microwave."

"You haven't even seen my new cabin because things have been so crazy with you."

"I know. Talk about a nightmare. To think that I came back home looking for peace and quiet."

He opened the truck door for her. "Well, you can relax now. It's all over. You should be able to move on with your life without looking back. I wanted to show off my cabin. If that's okay with you? We can stay in town if you'd prefer."

"How far away did you say it was?"

"Just about half an hour."

"That's actually perfect. I could use a little change of scenery."

Lily relaxed as they drove, with Jackson telling stories and the spring air blowing her hair through the open windows. She finally felt alive for the first time in a long time. Maybe everything would be okay after all. Yes, she'd still be alone, but that was her choice. She had Grace and a job she loved. Once the house was renovated, everything would be in place. She'd expand her business and stay busy. She hoped that the pain over parting ways with Rex would lessen with time.

When they pulled off onto the side road that wound up a big hill, Lily couldn't believe her eyes. Jackson's multistoried log cabin was magnificent. It was surrounded by a big green pasture on one side and what looked to be a forest filled with big trees and other foliage on the other.

"Wow, Jackson. This is amazing." Her eyes were drawn to the front porch and yard filled with beautiful flowers in bright spring colors of fuchsia, pink and yellow. "Are you a gardener now, too?"

"Do you like them?" he asked.

"Yes, they're gorgeous." She hopped out of the truck and took in another deep breath of air.

"Maybe you could photograph this place?"

"Oh, I'd love to. It's picture-perfect, Jackson. Completely beautiful and so tranquil. It feels as though we're the only people on the planet surrounded by this wondrous natural setting."

"I feel privileged to have you here and show you what I've done with the place."

"Have the others been out here yet?"

"No, you're the first one. I actually wanted to do a big reveal party here with everyone, but the timing hasn't been right. But having you here is good enough for me. Just seeing your reaction is priceless. You can go back and tell the others what they're missing out on."

She saw sadness in his big brown eyes. Reaching out, she grabbed on to his arm. "I'm so sorry. I realize I probably played a big part in messing up your plans. There's nothing stopping you now, though. I want you to have an epic housewarming party. You deserve it. You should be so proud of what you've done here. It's absolutely amazing."

"What's important, Lil, is that you're here now. I am excited to show you what I've done to the place."

"You haven't called me Lil in years." She laughed.

"It suits you." He motioned to her. "Come on in. Let me show you around." He opened up the front door, and she walked through it.

The inside wasn't nearly as put together yet as the outside, but that would take time. "Are you going to get Alison to help with the inside?"

"Of course. How can you have an interior designer as one of your best friends and not use them?"

She started looking around the first floor, jumping when Jackson's hand touched her back. "Sorry, you startled me. Honestly, I'm still a bit on edge after everything that happened."

"Hey, now. We both know you don't scare that easily." He gave her arm a light, playful punch.

"I'm a tough girl," she said.

"Especially after your time in the CIA."

Chills shot down her spine. "What?" she asked. How long had Jackson known about her being in the CIA? Did the others know, too?

He smiled. "Don't act so surprised, Lil. This is me you're talking with here. How many years have we known each other? Practically forever. There's no need to keep secrets at this point. Not between friends."

"Jackson, I'm so sorry. I hated keeping my work at the CIA from you and Alison and Guy. But you have to realize that my work was classified. I couldn't just go around telling everyone I was in the CIA. That would've been a big security risk." She took a breath. "I have to ask you, though. How exactly did you learn about my past?"

"It wasn't that difficult to dig around and find out what you had been up to those few years you spent in Washington, DC. You told all of us that you were working for the State Department, but that never added up to me. You didn't exactly fit the role of a diplomat. It explains why you were so secretive about your work and your time in DC."

"Well, I would appreciate it if you kept that knowledge to yourself. I wasn't planning on letting you all know until a few years down the road, once there was some distance between me and the work and I got the official okay from Langley."

"Are you worried about someone from your past finding out who you are?"

"Actually, yeah. I'd prefer to just focus on my photography. I left the CIA life behind."

"You left a lot behind, Lil."

"Oh, Jackson, where is this coming from?" She walked back into the living room and sat down on the couch.

"It's nothing. I shouldn't have brought it up." He went into the kitchen. "I'll go start dinner. Can I get you some iced tea while you wait?"

"Sure." She felt bad that Jackson thought she'd abandoned him. She wondered if all her friends felt that way. Probably so. Now that she was safe, she needed to make a concerted effort to spend more quality time with them. "Jackson, I know I haven't been a great friend."

"Don't say it like that. You had a job to do for your country. I get that, even if it still hurt to be shut out for so long." He walked into the living room carrying a large glass of tea. "I know you like it sweet." He handed her the drink.

She took a large sip. "This is delicious. Thank you." She paused. "You don't have to go through all that trouble cooking on your own. I can help you. I'm not totally incompetent if you give me precise directions."

He shook his head. "I've got the cooking under

control. There are other things I'd like to talk about with you, though."

"What do you mean?"

"Remember in high school when I asked you on a date and you told me no? That we were better off as friends?"

"That was a long time ago." She looked up at him. "Why are you asking about that?"

"How would you feel if I asked you that same question now?"

Whoa. She hadn't seen that coming. Did Jackson think this was a date? She needed to head this off before he went down that road any further. "Jackson, I'm not currently in any position to answer that."

He cocked his head to the side. "Really? Because it seemed as if you and the FBI agent were super close."

She shook her head. "It wasn't like that at all. He was just doing his job. He had to stick close to me because there was a psychotic serial killer out there trying to hunt me down." She took another sip of tea, enjoying the sweetness combined with the tang of lemon.

He took a seat beside her. "If that's true, then maybe there is some hope for us."

"Jackson, you really could do so much better than me. I can't offer you what you need."

"But I want to be with you, Lil. Always have."

"What? What do you mean you always have?" Her head started to pound. She tried to take a few deep breaths but realized it was becoming harder to get air.

She looked down at the tea and then back up at him as he stared at her. "Jackson, no."

"Yes, Lil," he said in a perfectly calm voice.

Recognition hit her like a freight train. "No, not you."

"I give you about five or so minutes before you're out cold from the special concoction I prepared for you. It's similar to what I used on your pizza. When Sean stopped by to check on me, he didn't think anything of leaving me alone with the food while he conducted a security sweep of my place. I actually miscalculated and put too much on your pizza. I was more careful this time, though."

As her world started closing in on her, she fought to get answers. If she was going to die, she had to know. "Did you really kill all of those women?"

"Yes," he answered without any hesitation.

"But why? I don't understand why you'd do all of this."

"Because of you, Lil. It's always been about you." He reached out and put his hand on her knee. "You don't think I randomly picked women who looked like you, did you?" He shook his head. "No. I had a plan. But you messed it up. From the moment you came back into town. It was supposed to be you and me back together again. Like we were always meant to be."

"You haven't asked me on a date since I've been home."

"Because I could tell that you weren't interested. But just having you back in my life, I honestly couldn't control my need to be with you. So I discovered my talent for finding what ended up being very poor substitutes for you. Once I started down that road, though, I realized how much I enjoyed taking those lives. It was as if I was born to kill those women."

In a fog, she kept talking. "It was you in my house that first night, wasn't it?"

"Yes. There was never any hired gun. That was all part of my manipulation of the evidence to set up Sean and make that theory plausible. And that night is actually what caused me to delve into your background. You fought me off like a trained warrior. Imagine my surprise when I found out you were a CIA agent. But that only added to your mystique in my eyes. An even greater challenge and more wonderful prize than I ever imagined. Although, I'll never again make the mistake of underestimating your strength. You're clearly a worthy opponent. None of the other women I killed even came close. Most cried and gave up. It was so easy to take their lives. To watch them take their final breaths. To know that I had the power to decide if they lived or died. It was such a big thrill. Nothing in the world is like it."

She couldn't even begin to fathom everything she was hearing. The man she had known since he was just a boy—the man who she had grown up with, whom she considered one of her only true friends in the world—was a serial killer. And he was going to murder her. She feared that it wouldn't be fast, that he might have torture in mind. Would Rex put two and two together and find her? An overwhelming feeling of regret washed over her. She never should've shut Rex out. Now she was probably going to die without having told Rex her true feelings for him. All because she was afraid. Fighting to stay awake, she turned her attention back to Jackson.

"At any rate, I never planned on really hurting you that night at your house. I actually wanted to bring you here with me. And have us work on a relationship together. It seemed like the most prudent thing to do."

"Prudent?" She realized that Jackson was totally delusional.

"Yes, but when that aspect of my plan failed, I realized that I would have to take more drastic action."

"Like shooting Rex or trying to burn down my house with me in it."

"It's all okay now, Lil. You're here. Just like it was always meant to be. There's no reason for you to be concerned about anything else."

"What about Sean?" That poor man was innocent of all wrongdoing.

He shrugged. "He was a convenient scapegoat. I had nothing against Sean personally. He had no interest in you that I could tell."

"He confessed to all of the murders."

"Because I threatened to kill his family if he didn't give a detailed confession. I provided the information through a letter. He never knew who I was. Just that he had no choice but to make the false confession or that I would kill them. He obviously knew I wasn't kidding, because I included details of the murders only the real killer would know."

She tried to form more words, but nothing came out. She could feel herself fading as her body sank deeper into the sofa. *Dear Lord, I need You now.*

Lily hadn't responded to Rex's texts or calls since last night. He didn't like being completely shut out of her life. Yeah, she'd wanted her space. And yeah, she'd made it clear that she needed some time. But he refused to take that as her final answer. And he doubted she would be the type to just give him the silent treatment or ignore his calls completely. He didn't think he was coming across as that pushy.

When his phone finally rang, he was excited, thinking that it had to be her. But then he realized he didn't recognize the number. His heart sank.

"Hello," he said.

"Is this Rex?" a female voice asked.

"Yes. Who is this?"

"It's Alison. Lily's friend."

Immediately his gut clenched. Something was wrong. "What is it?"

"It's about Lily. She went out last night and never came home."

"What? What do you mean she didn't come home?"

"I didn't want to sound the alarm for no reason, but it's not like her to go this long without texting or calling. I had a client dinner to go to so she decided to meet up with Jackson. When she didn't come home, I thought she'd crashed at his place. But I walked down to his house and no one was there. I'm worried they got into an accident or something."

"You said that she was with Jackson? Are you absolutely sure that she was with him?"

"I left for dinner before she did, but that was the plan. He was going to come pick her up and take her out."

"And you've tried Jackson, too?"

"Yes. No answer from him, either."

"Alison, I'm going to ask you something, and I need you to think carefully before you answer."

"Okay."

"Do you know if Jackson has ever had any interest in Lily that goes beyond friendship?"

"Well, he definitely crushed on her hard in high school. I think she was totally oblivious to it. But since we have been adults, if he has romantic feelings for her, he hasn't mentioned it to me." She paused. "You're beginning to frighten me, Rex. What are implying?"

"I'm just trying to consider the big picture."

"Jackson wouldn't hurt Lily, if that's what you're thinking. He loves her. We're a tight-knit group. The three of us have known each other since we were children. There's just—there's just no way."

"I want to make sure I get all the facts from you right now."

Then he heard Alison start to cry. "You're serious, aren't you? Jackson is a killer? He murdered all those women? And maybe even Lily, too?" Her voice cracked as she spoke.

That was exactly what Rex was afraid of. "Alison, just sit tight. Let me make some calls and get back to you."

"All right."

"Oh, one more thing. Where is Grace?"

"She's here with me. She's fine."

"Thanks. I'll call you back."

Rex knew that Lily wouldn't have left Grace overnight without letting Alison know. He called Derrick immediately and filled him in on the situation. As he spoke to Derrick, he jogged out to his car and started driving. He had to get to the prison quickly. Something was terribly off. There was a missing piece of information, and he felt that Sean would be the one to have it.

After pulling some strings and working with Derrick, Rex was able to get in front of Sean, even though he was technically on leave from the FBI.

Across the prison glass, Rex looked into Sean's eyes and saw what he already knew. "You made a false confession. Didn't you? Why?"

Sean looked down and back up. "I'm so sorry. But the killer threatened my kid sister and her newborn baby. And my mother. Said he would butcher them all into a million pieces. I had no choice." Tears filled Sean's eyes. "I couldn't let that happen to them. Not if there was something I could do to stop it. I knew what that guy was capable of, so I didn't want to test him."

"Who is he?" Rex asked.

Sean shook his head. "I don't know. My attorney

brought me the letter during one of our visits to discuss my case. It was in a sealed envelope."

"Did your attorney know what was in the letter?"

"No. And I just assumed the note was from my family because the killer had put their return address on it. That indicated that this madman knew exactly where my family lived. It wasn't an idle threat. Either I confessed or my loved ones would be killed."

Rex had to admit it was a brilliant strategy on the killer's part. All roads led to Jackson, but he needed to get out of that prison and start tracking him down. If he wasn't already too late.

TWELVE

Lily awoke with a strange taste in her mouth. Then she realized that she had been gagged. She tried to move, but Jackson had tied her to a chair with her arms behind her back. Her body ached all over and her neck was stiff. She had no concept of time and how long she had been out.

She looked at her surroundings and instantly knew she was in the basement of the log cabin. There were no windows and no visible exits, except up the steps to the main floor. Immediately, she started working on the ropes that bound her ankles and wrists. She'd been trained in techniques to get out of situations just like this. But she would need a little time, and her escape would be contingent on the strength of the knots. There was no way she was giving up without a fight. She hadn't made it this far to die in a basement at the hands of a man she'd thought was a friend but was actually a cold-blooded killer. She'd now been terribly wrong about two men in her life. Well, at least she'd been right about Rex. Would she ever see him again?

Lord, I'm going to fight my hardest to get out of here, but if I don't make it out alive, I want to make sure I'm right with You. I know I turned away from You and hardened my heart. But I want to walk with You again. I want an opportunity to grow my faith. Yet, if this is the plan You have for me, I can accept it. Just please forgive me.

She let out a deep breath and started to think. While she was relieved to know that she'd been right about Sean, she was horrified to think that Jackson was the killer. Had he really been hung up on her all these years? The look in his eyes had been one of total delusion. And as much as she hated to believe it, there had also been an evil gleam. One that she'd never seen from him before.

Jackson had been the kid who was a friend to everyone. And as an adult, he seemed totally put together. A solid job, a tight circle of friends. He was compassionate and helpful. Now she felt the man who had done this was a total stranger.

"You're awake."

She looked up to see Jackson walking down the steps and into the basement.

"Jackson, we need to talk," she said. She didn't even know where she was going to go with this, but she had to do something before it was too late.

"I agree."

He seemed so calm right now, as if they were about to have a friendly chat over coffee. Just like old times. Except that nothing was like it used to be. Her life, even if there wasn't much of it left on this earth, had been forever changed by this man.

"I was a bit overbearing last night." He pulled one of the other wooden chairs directly in front of her and took a seat.

She started putting the pieces together and realized it must only be the next day. Maybe morning? Or later? One thing she knew was that she had to keep him talking. She had to buy time in hopes that Rex would find her. It was a long shot, but it was the best she had. She felt she could take Jackson in hand-to-hand combat, but tied up she was practically helpless. She needed more time to work on the ropes.

"I should've given you the opportunity to really tell me how you feel about me," he said. He reached out and touched her cheek, and she didn't flinch. She couldn't let him see her sweat. And she definitely couldn't act repulsed by him. If she needed to play a part right now to stay alive, she was going to give it her best shot. Her CIA training would get her through this. It had to.

"You're one of my oldest and dearest friends, Jackson. You understand that, right?"

"You know, I was mad about you leaving after college and going completely off the grid. Never calling or anything. But once I learned about your CIA career, I was able to forgive that."

"Thank you," she said. "I'm sorry that I had to break off most contacts. It was just easier that way. And safer for all of you."

He nodded. "But what I don't understand is how you could've chosen the FBI agent over me."

She needed to keep her cool. "Like I told you before, Jackson, there is absolutely nothing going on between me and Rex."

"I want to believe that, Lil. I really do." He looked down at his watch and frowned. "We're going to have to leave the cabin soon. It's only a matter of time before Alison starts to worry about you and the FBI gets onto our trail."

"What's the endgame here? Where are you going to take me?"

"Don't worry about all of those details. Rest assured, I've planned for every contingency. You'll be well taken care of."

"If you want to be with me, then why do you have me tied up? That's not exactly a way to make me feel loved."

He cocked his head to the side. "We're way past love, Lil. You've forced me to do awful things. Kill so many people. All because of you. And now you're going to have to pay for that by dealing with some rules and regulations that I have put in place to make sure that we can be together."

She swallowed and contemplated her next move in this chess game. She let some silence pass between them before asking, "What do you want from me?"

He smiled. "I want you, Lil. All of you. Forever. You're mine and no one else's now."

"Will you stop hurting other women now that you have me?"

"That's really none of your concern."

"Please, Jackson. If you care for me like you say you do, then you'll do as I ask and stop the killing."

His hand connected with her face before she even registered the hard slap. She recoiled. She hadn't expected this violent outburst from him. And then just as she was catching her breath and trying to compose herself, he hit her again. Hard. She tasted the tinge of blood in her mouth.

As she made eye contact with him she felt that he might just finish her off right then and there. She steadied herself as she waited for the next blow.

"Why did you make me do that, Lil?" He stood up and started pacing. "You're always making me do these things I don't really want to do."

She didn't respond.

"Now you're bleeding!"

It was at that moment that Lily realized she'd made good progress on the ropes around her ankles and her wrists.

He walked away from her, and she quickly kept maneuvering out of the ankle ropes and wrist ties until they were both loosened enough for her to break out of.

A few minutes later, he strode back into the room with a washcloth in hand. His mental illness was evident. Hitting her one moment and trying to take care of her the next. But she was smart enough to know that the ending Jackson had planned would be a deadly one. She had to fight back if there was any chance of getting out of this alive.

When he crouched down in front of her and placed the warm washcloth on her lip, she took a deep breath, sending up a prayer for help.

This was the opportunity she needed. She delivered a swift, hard kick upward to his groin. He fell over on the ground and moaned. She didn't waste a second.

She ran as fast as she could up the stairs and out of the cabin.

Rex had picked up Derrick and now they were speeding down the road. Jackson had once offered up his cabin to Lily to use as a safe place. Rex was now banking on the fact that Jackson would've taken her there. Alison didn't know the exact location, but she did know the time frame for when Jackson had bought it and the FBI was able to run a property search to determine the cabin's location.

Rex only prayed that they wouldn't be too late.

"She's going to be okay, man," Derrick said, attempting to reassure him.

"I appreciate you saying that, but you and I both know that she's in the hands of a psychotic serial killer." Rex accelerated his already fast pace as he said those words. "Even a minute could make the difference between Lily living or dying."

"I still can't believe what he did to Sean. And that Sean went along with it."

"If he'd threatened to kill your family, including an innocent child, you would've done the same thing."

"You're probably right. It's an awful scenario any

way you look at it." Derrick checked the GPS. "We're about fifteen minutes out."

Rex planned to cut that down to ten. Now they seemed to be in the middle of nowhere, weaving through the Georgia countryside. It was amazing how rural it could get just half an hour outside the city.

"This area appears to include a lot of farmland," Derrick said.

"Perfect place for a serial killer," Rex said, not hiding his sarcasm. "I still can't believe I didn't even consider Jackson. I sat across from him at the kitchen table. I interviewed him. Asked him questions about his friendship with Lily, and I never saw it coming."

"No one did. We were all off base. No one ever considered that Lily was actually the impetus for the killing to start. We just assumed she was just like any of the other victims."

"If something happens to her, Derrick, I don't know how I'll be able to shoulder that type of pain and guilt."

"Don't think like that. None of this is your fault."

"It sure feels as though it is." He'd replayed every single interaction with Jackson over and over in his mind, trying to figure out how he could've missed the signs. "I should've put together the connection. He should've at least been on my radar. But he just seemed so benign. He showed what I thought was genuine concern for her well-being, as any real friend would."

"Like I said, he had us all fooled."

"That doesn't provide me much solace if she's dead."

"Don't talk like that." Derrick paused. "Take this next turn on your right. We're almost there."

Rex didn't take his eyes off the road as they sped down the street that led to a large multistoried cabin. It certainly didn't look like a serial killer's den. Bright blooming flowers lined the front yard. The main house was flanked by a smaller barn off to one side and a wooded area on the other.

"Don't hesitate to use whatever force necessary to take this guy out," Derrick said.

"You don't have to remind me of that." *Lord, please let Lily be alive and unharmed.* He stopped the car and jumped out, gun drawn. He wasn't taking any chances.

They ran toward the cabin and saw that the front door was wide-open. "Let's clear this house ASAP." He rushed down the basement steps fearing the worst—afraid that he'd find Lily's dead body. But what he found gave him hope.

He saw a chair and ropes. Also blood speckled on the floor. Had he tied her up? Had she gotten away?

Then the dreaded thought came to him that they were too late. That Jackson had taken her and was long gone.

Derrick joined him in the basement. "The rest of the cabin is clear."

"Look at this."

"There was a struggle here," Derrick said. "Maybe she was able to get away."

"Or she tried to fight him off and he took her to another location?"

"We can't do much about it if he's already on the road. We'll have to radio that in. But since his truck is still here, it's most likely that they are both here, unless he had another vehicle. Backup is about fifteen minutes out. We can canvass the area until they get here."

"We need the search-and-rescue canines out here," Rex said. "This property is huge."

"They're en route," Derrick said. "I requested them as we were leaving because of the rural setting."

"I'm not going to wait on them, though." He jogged back up the steps and walked through the cabin with Derrick right behind him. Rex exited the front door and started his search.

"If I were her, I would've headed toward the woods," Rex said. "It would provide Lily with much more cover. If she headed west, she'd encounter wide-open fields and the road, making her an easy target." If she'd been able to get away unharmed, Rex felt Lily could hold her own against Jackson, given her extensive training. But that was a lot of ifs.

Right now he had to try to keep his head on straight and not lose hope. There was no time for second-guessing. If Lily was in those woods, he was going to find her.

Keeping up a solid pace, Lily ran like the wind, her arms and legs aching from her overnight ordeal. She'd never been more thankful for all of her physical training, and hoped she could outrun Jackson. Or at least put distance in between them. That was her first objective.

Well, her first objective was to stay alive. But after that she needed a plan. Each minute that she kept breathing, she felt more motivated to survive. She wasn't going to give up.

As she ran, she also kept her eyes open for a suitable hideout that would give her good visibility, but so far, no luck. The hilly terrain was jagged, with tons of rocks and branches. This hot pursuit reminded her of one of her first missions with the CIA when she'd got on the wrong side of a foreign asset. She prayed this ended the same way as that chase had. With her getting away safely.

Her heart thumped loudly in her chest as her feet pounded into the damp ground.

By the time she heard the footsteps gaining on her, it was too late.

Jackson tackled her hard from behind. Hitting the ground covered in twigs, branches and rocks with full force, she tasted the grit of dirt in her mouth.

She didn't know what kind of weapon Jackson had, but it didn't matter. She was going to fight for her life even at gunpoint because that was her only alternative. There was no way that Lily was going to let Jackson take her back to the cabin or his truck.

Rolling over, she pushed him off her using all her strength. Jackson was taller and outweighed her by at least fifty pounds, but it was obvious that he wasn't a trained fighter. She sprang to her feet and instead of trying to engage in direct combat, she started running again.

"Lil, don't make me end it this way," he yelled.

Then she heard the sound of gunshots. Much too close for comfort. She did her best to run in random patterns to try to avoid getting shot in the back. But she refused to stop because she couldn't risk getting shot at point-blank range. Even if Jackson wasn't a great shot, the closer he was, the better his chance of hitting her. This method at least gave her a chance to get away.

Her heart pounded as adrenaline surged through her body. In her efforts to try to avoid getting shot, she didn't notice the uneven drop-off in the ground until it was too late. She fell into the pit and knew she'd made a deadly mistake.

Lily tried to adjust her eyes to the darkness of the pit. The light from outside still shone down, but she couldn't see the full hole in great detail. Only what was directly in front of her. The rest was shaded. She felt around her to determine if there was anything she could hold on to if she attempted to climb out. But there was nothing.

"I know you're down there, Lil," Jackson said.

She could see his menacing shadow above her. But she had to wonder, if he came down, how would they get out? Then a shiver went down her back. What if that was his plan? What if he didn't want to get out? They'd die down there in that dark, muddy hole together.

No, Lord. Please don't let that happen.

Her thoughts then went to Rex. And how she'd pushed him away time and again. Instead of accepting the love and affection that he was trying to offer her. Love? Was that what real love felt like?

While her last thoughts on earth might be of Rex and what could've been, she had to at least attempt to get out of this mess, even though it seemed impossible. If Jackson wanted to, he could reach down with his gun, aim and shoot her right now. She had nowhere to run. She pushed her body as close as possible up against the wall of the pit to try to stay out of the line of fire, but it wouldn't take him long to shift angles and get a direct shot.

"Jackson, don't come down here. If you do, you won't be able to get back out. We'll be trapped in this pit. You don't want that, do you?"

"Let me worry about that."

"This isn't the way you pictured us being together. You need to think about this." If he was going to jump down into the pit, it would give her a split-second opportunity to get the upper hand right when he landed. Clenching her fists, she waited for him to make a move.

A couple of moments passed and she took a few deep breaths in anticipation of the fight that was about to take place.

Jackson jumped down into the hole, which she estimated was about a ten-foot drop. There was room down there for a couple of people to stand, but that was about it.

As soon as his feet touched the ground, she leaped

into action and delivered a hard right kick to his ribs. He groaned and stumbled back a step. He started to reach for his gun, but she connected with another strong kick to his side.

Not waiting for him to recover, she rammed her right hand as hard as she could into his nose and heard the crunching sound of breaking bones. She got no pleasure out of hurting him, even after all the atrocities he had committed. But she also realized that this was her only chance to take him out before he killed her. Time was not on her side.

He looked at her and she didn't even recognize the man standing in front of her with blood gushing down his face. And just like that he rushed her, pure evil in his dark eyes, tackling her hard to the ground. She found it impossible to breathe as his two-hundred-plus pounds pinned her to the ground.

He reared back and slapped her hard across the face. Clearly, she'd angered him, and he continued his assault. This man was seeking revenge against her. She took a pummeling, but through each blow she desperately tried to focus on surviving. On getting out. Alive. She felt that the Lord would answer her prayers. Even if it just meant that he'd spare her from torture before death.

But in that moment, she couldn't help but cry out in pain.

"It wasn't supposed to end like this, Lil," Jackson said. But he didn't stop his onslaught against her. With every strike, the pain intensified throughout her body, but her will to live didn't fade. She continued to focus on pushing through the pain.

"You should've come to me willingly. You should've loved me the way I loved you. This is all your fault. We could've been happy together. You stole that from me."

Garnering every ounce of strength she had and praying to God for a miraculous intervention, she was able to push him off her, managing to roll to the side. But then he was right there again. Dragging her to her feet by the hair.

"Don't do this, Jackson. You don't have to take another life. Look me in the eyes and tell me that you really want me dead."

"You just don't understand, do you? This is our destiny. It was always meant to be just you and me, Lil. Only the two of us in our own world."

"Jackson, you need to get a grip. We'll die down here. It won't be the two of us living a happy life together. We'll be dead."

"Don't say things like that, Lil. You're going to be mine forever, just like I've planned for years."

She took a deep breath, and then the sound of a single gunshot rang loudly through the air. Jackson crumpled to the ground right in front of her. It was a direct shot to the back of the head.

She realized then that she had been screaming and tears were flowing down her face. The mixture of tears and blood stung her wounds.

"Lily, are you all right?" Rex called out.

"Yes. But I can't get out of here. There's no way for me to climb up."

"Is Jackson dead?"

She looked down at the body. Unmoving and covered in blood. There was no doubt that the gunshot wound to the head would've been lethal. "Yes, he's dead."

"Hang tight. We've got a rope. We're going to rappel down and bring you back up."

"Okay." She tried to steady herself. To process what had just happened. She started shaking, not just from the emotional trauma but also the pain that was undeniable.

Lily was in a daze as the FBI team rappelled down the hole and hoisted her out effortlessly.

Once out of the small pit, she saw Rex standing there, his eyes wide with concern. Unable to help herself, she threw her arms around Rex's neck. He held on to her tightly.

"Lily, I am so sorry."

"You couldn't have known. He was my friend for years and I had no clue." She sucked in a breath, trying not to hyperventilate. "Rex, he killed all of those women because of me. All because of me. I don't even know how to deal with that."

"This isn't on you, Lily. Jackson obviously had major psychological issues. You aren't to blame for the deaths of those women. You did everything in your power and then some to stop him. If anything, I should be the one apologizing. The FBI never even considered the fact that you were the killer's main focus. We just assumed he wanted to kill you because you thwarted his attempt on your life. That you were one of many on his list. That could've been a deadly mistake."

"I'm just thankful that I'm alive, Rex. Even as I mourn for all those other innocent women."

"You need medical attention right away. You're hurt."

"I know. But just hold me for another minute, will you?" She wouldn't hide her heart any longer. No, she had serious feelings for this man. Feelings unlike anything she'd ever experienced before.

She pulled back after a minute and looked up into his big brown eyes. Her tears started again, and she couldn't even form words as the emotions bubbled up inside her.

"I know," he said. "I feel the same way."

Except he didn't shed any tears. No, he was her rock right now and she held on to him tightly.

"I prayed so hard that I would be saved," she said. "God answered my prayers. He heard me, Rex."

"Lily, God was always ready to answer your prayers. The answers He gives may not be exactly what we want to hear. But He was with us today. I knew for certain that it wasn't time for you to leave this earth. Not yet. And I'm so thankful to Him for that."

"I'm thankful, too. I didn't want to contemplate dying having not been honest with you about how I felt. I know I erected some huge walls around my heart, and provided excuses about why we shouldn't pursue our feelings for each other. But the truth is that I was just afraid. I was terrified of being hurt again."

"And I'm terrified at the thought of living my life without you in it, Lily."

"Really?" she asked.

"Yes. You're the most unique person I've ever met. Stronger than most agents I've worked with, but with a kind and gentle heart. I know it's soon and things have been crazy because of what you've gone through, but I want to give us a chance."

"I do, too. More than you can even imagine."

"Good. Because somewhere along the line, I've fallen in love with you, Lily. The kind of love that I think only comes along once in a lifetime."

"I believe that, too. The Lord brought you into my life for a reason. Not just to literally save my life, but to help lead me back to my faith. And to show me what true love really is."

He leaned down and pressed his lips to hers in a kiss sweeter than any she'd ever known. And this time she kissed him back without reservation and with an open heart. In that moment she wasn't thinking about her past, but only her bright future with Rex.

EPILOGUE

Lily sat on her back porch watching Rex throw the tennis balls for Grace, who was having the time of her life romping around the backyard. She picked up her camera and took a few action shots as the two ran around.

The past six months had been a time of healing and rebuilding. Her house had finally been renovated after the fire. It truly felt like home now—especially when she had Rex over. He'd held her when she was weak and kissed her when she felt strong. He'd literally been by her side each step of this long road to gaining her life back.

Learning the details about Jackson's master plan had been difficult for her. Jackson had kept records on his laptop documenting everything. He had chosen Sean as the scapegoat because he was a rookie cop. He'd taken advantage of all the computer training and resources that the tech company he worked for provided. He'd been able to plant or manipulate all the evidence to frame Sean. It still boggled her mind that Jackson had become a killer, but she was trying to move forward.

Rex jogged up the back porch steps with Grace right by his side. A bright smile lit up his face. And she felt the same way. She'd never been happier.

Grace dropped the ball in front of her. "I think we're done playing for a bit, Grace." But she leaned down to pick the ball up, and that was when she realized it felt odd.

"Is this the new ball you bought for Grace at the pet store the other day?"

"Yes, but there's something in there for you," Rex said.

"For me?" What could he be talking about? Curious, she twisted the top of the ball off and then her breath caught. There was a black velvet ring box inside.

He pulled her up from her seat and dropped to one knee, taking the box out of her hands and opening it. The princess-cut solitaire diamond sparkled in the fall sunshine. Her heart pounded.

"Lily Parker, you're everything to me. I realize now why I waited to find someone special. And it was because I was waiting for the Lord to send you to me. You challenge me, you make me laugh and you warm my heart with your love and generosity. Would you make me the happiest man on the earth and marry me?"

Lily could barely form words. But she also knew that there were some things she wanted to say. "Rex, I was so hurt from what happened to me in the past. But when I'm with you, I'm not looking back. I'm not stuck in the pain and regret that swallowed me whole for so long. I can see us having a life together, and that makes me so happy."

He smiled. "Is that a yes?"

She nodded, now trying to fight off the happy tears. "That's a definite yes."

He slid the diamond on her finger and Grace barked loudly with excitement.

She looked up into his eyes and knew that her life would never be the same. She'd found what she never thought really existed. A family for her and Grace.

"Can Grace be in the wedding?" she asked.

"I wouldn't want it any other way," he said.

As he sealed their proposal with a lingering kiss, she held on to the man who had made her have faith again in all aspects of her life. And she knew that she was truly loved.

* * * * *

Dear Reader,

Thank you for reading *Picture Perfect Murder*! It was enjoyable and a challenge to write a complex character like Lily. A woman who had lived through life-and-death situations as a CIA agent, and then faced an entirely different threat back at home. Lily's life shows that we can be complicated, multifaceted people with a lot of different interests—and a lot of different problems. Lily's story is special to me because I feel it shows that no matter what you've been through, the Lord is ready to take you back with open arms. And that He's been there each step of the way with us even when we may have had our doubts.

And, of course, I don't think I can write a story without a furry companion. I hope you enjoyed Grace the lovable rescue Labrador as much as I did. Animals provide so much comfort and joy to us, especially when we are at our weakest.

I love to hear from readers! You can visit my website at www.racheldylan.com or email me at racheldylanauthor@gmail.com.

Rachel Dylan

SPECIAL EXCERPT FROM

Love Inspired
SUSPENSE

*A military medic and a rookie K-9 officer find a
connection in the midst of a drug crisis in Desert Valley.*

*Read on for an excerpt from
TRUTH AND CONSEQUENCES,
the next exciting book in the captivating
K-9 cop miniseries, **ROOKIE K-9 UNIT**,
available May 2016 from Love Inspired Suspense.*

"Get out of here. Now."

David Evans glanced up at the man holding a gun on
him and then glanced down at the bleeding man lying on
the floor of the passenger train. "I'm not leaving. I'm a
doctor, and this man needs help."

The gunman who had just stabbed the train attendant
glanced at his buddy, agitation obvious as he shuffled
sideways on the narrow aisle.

David had seen the whole attack from the doorway
of his seat a few feet up the aisle. While the two argued
about leaving without the packages of drugs they'd
dropped, David had hurried to help the injured man.

But before they got away, the two possible drug
couriers had spotted David moving up the aisle.

"You better keep traveling, mister, if you want to live.
I'll finish off both of you if either of you talk."

David held his breath and stayed there on his knees
while the two men rushed off the train.

"I'm a medic," he told the shocked older man. "I'm going to help you, okay?"

The pale-faced man nodded. "He stabbed me."

"I saw," David said. "Just lie still while I examine you. Help should be on the way."

When he heard sirens, he breathed a sigh of relief.

He'd come here searching for a woman he didn't really know, except in his imagination. But a promise was a promise. He wasn't leaving Desert Valley without finding her.

When he looked up a few minutes later to see a pretty female officer with long blond hair coming toward him, a sleek tan-and-white canine pulling on a leash in front of her, David thought he must be dreaming.

He knew that face. While he sat on the cold train floor holding a bloody shirt to a man who was about to pass out, he looked up and into the vivid blue eyes of the woman he'd traveled here to find. Whitney Godwin was coming to his aid.

Don't miss
TRUTH AND CONSEQUENCES by Lenora Worth,
available May 2016 wherever
Love Inspired® Suspense books and ebooks are sold.

www.LoveInspired.com